A Colt for the Kid

Johnnie Callum was a half-grown boy when Donovan's riders stamped his parents' homestead flat and sent him running terrified into the night. He ran far and fast over the trackless range that was Donovan's empire and fetched up in the hands of Josh Manders, a brutal sheepherder.

Manders worked him hard and in six years came near to breaking Johnnie's spirit. But not near enough. Finally, there came a day when Johnnie's resentment took charge and his big, bony hands wrapped around Manders' throat in an unshakable hold.

Johnnie took Manders' horse and then worked for Sam Stevens. But when Donovan was all set up to wipe out Stevens' ranch Johnnie began to get gun-minded!

A Colt for the Kid

JOHN SAUNDERS

A Black Horse Western

ROBERT HALE · LONDON

© John Saunders 1960
First published 1960
This edition published in Great Britain 2009

ISBN 978-0-7090-8792-2

Robert Hale Limited
Clerkenwell House
Clerkenwell Green
London EC1R 0HT

www.halebooks.com

Typeset by
Derek Doyle & Associates, Shaw Heath
Printed and bound in Great Britain by
CPI Antony Rowe, Chippenham and Eastbourne

CHAPTER ONE

Josh Manders was the sheepherder's name; a dried up, stringy, brutish man with his unshaven chin and dirt-grimed face. He worked his flocks on the banks of the San Juan river, keeping, for the most part, to the mountainous country where he was unlikely to run into cattlemen. For help he had an eighteen-year-old youth, Johnnie Callum. Johnnie was tall, his blond hair bleached near white and was angular of frame. He was almost permanently hungry, and had for Manders the hatred of a slave for his master. Yet in a way, he clung to Manders as being his only source of life. It was Manders who decided when they should eat, where they should sleep and when they should move on.

They were on the move now, had been since dawn, herding the hundreds of complaining woollies higher into the hills. Johnnie, astride a horse whose every bone could be counted, was saddle-sore almost beyond endurance. He kept glancing at the red rim of the sun now just on the point of dipping, and wondered if the old man would ever call a halt. He considered Manders, who was just forty, to be very ancient, and for that reason did not resent the fact that he had done all the chasing after stray bunches of sheep while Manders had ridden at an easy walk behind the flock.

Nevertheless, Johnnie's consideration for Manders' age in no way whittled down his hatred for the man. That hatred was of too long a standing. Six years, in fact, although Johnnie could not have stated the day precisely. He had vague and frightening memories of the day Manders had found him wandering in the vast triangle made by the Colorado and San Juan rivers. Johnnie had spent most of the previous night wailing for his father and mother, both of whom he believed to be dead. He would have continued wailing on the following morning, but Manders was a man of little patience and no feeling, and had belted Johnnie into silence. There had been frequent use of the belt ever since and a continual dinning into the boy that he ought to be grateful for being found and kept safely from the murderous hands of Mark Donovan.

Johnnie knew, or thought he knew, about Donovan. He was the biggest rancher for hundreds of miles around and drove homesteaders and sheepmen from his range without a hint of mercy in the process.

Seth and Louise Callum, Johnnie's parents, had been homesteaders on what Donovan considered to be his land, and on a dark night Donovan's men had swooped on the homestead in a yelling, gunfiring mob. The Callums had been dragged from their beds, the soddy demolished and the growing crops stamped flat. In the stark terror that had swamped Johnnie, he had fled into the night, running aimlessly, falling often, going anywhere so long as he got away from the horror that drove him nearly frantic. When Manders found him, he was twenty or more miles from the wreck of his home and the sheepherder who was driving his flock away from the district, took him further and further each succeeding day. In the following weeks and months, Johnnie's memories of home and parents dimmed, beaten from him by Manders' cruel usage of him. Fear and hatred

6

of the man grew but now the fear was diminishing and the hatred growing. Growing because Johnnie was beginning to realize his youthful strength and still thought of Manders as a very old man.

Manders reached his objective with the very last of the daylight, a blind canyon, narrow of entrance and rimmed with almost sheer cliffs. He bawled to Johnnie:

'Get 'em in the canyon, darn your lazy hide. Come on, swing after that bunch of strays. We ain't got all night.'

Without answering back, Johnnie kicked his mount to a faster pace, turned the strays towards the entrance then rounded up another bunch that broke free from the main flock.

In all, it was near to half an hour before he had sent the last sheep bleating its way into the canyon then he rode to where Manders was seated on the ground.

'You've been a hell of a time,' Manders said. 'Get the fire going.'

Obediently, Johnnie climbed from the saddle and went to gather brushwood. It was in his mind that Manders could have lit the fire instead of sitting idly, but he knew that a protest would only have brought abuse and perhaps blows. He got back with the kindling and started to pile it in a neat pyramid. Manders was still sprawled on the ground but he had taken a whiskey bottle from his pack and had it to his mouth. When he lowered it he glared at Johnnie's back and an ugly sneer twisted his mouth. He was beginning to despise the kid with a passion that turned his stomach. Beginning to wish that he had left him where he had found him. He took another swig at the bottle and the hot liquor filled him with a killing anger, blotting from his mind the fact that, for six years Johnnie had worked for him without payment, remembering only that there had been two mouths to fill. As the whiskey fumes eddied his brain he magnified the cost of the boy's keep until it became a vast amount of money. Then suddenly he could contain his rage no longer. He lashed out with the toe of his boot at Johnnie's bent back and sent him floundering over the newly kindled blaze.

The boy gave a scream of pain as the flames seared his chest and neck. He got to his feet half blinded, and made a stumbling rush at the sheepherder. From his seated position Manders met the rush with a further thrust of his foot right at the pit of Johnnie's stomach. Again the boy went down, this time rolling in agony. Manders got to his feet, moved to Johnnie's side and drove his boot deliberately at the boy's ribs. He got in three kicks then something in Johnnie snapped. He grappled Manders by the ankles and threw him to the ground then rolled on top of him. He pounded at Manders' face with his unskilled but strong fists. Manders, astonished at the sudden change in the boy and hurt by the thudding blows, kicked, rolled and squirmed until he was free. He got to his feet and backed away, clawing at the heavy belt he wore.

'Yer young snake,' he howled. 'I'll cut yer to ribbons for that.'

He fully expected Johnnie to turn and run but instead he had to cope with the boy's head down charge and flailing arms. He dodged to one side, got his belt free and swung the buckle end at Johnnie's head. The blow opened an inch or so of the boy's scalp and Manders, determined to teach him a lesson, swung the leather again. This time a gash appeared in the boy's cheek but instead of retreating he bored unskilfully at the man and wrapped him with his arms. For a minute or two the pair wrestled then Manders fell to the ground. Awkwardly, Johnnie got astride of him and grabbed both hands into Manders' unkempt hair. In spite of the blood streaming into his eyes and Manders' savage efforts to break free he raised Manders' head from the ground and smashed it remorsely down again.

Manders knew real fear when his head struck the unyielding ground for a second time. He let out a screaming: 'No, Johnnie, don't.' Then as his head hit again, a fainter: 'Johnnie, oh my God, no.'

Johnnie smashed Manders to the ground several times more before his mind reacted to the fact that the man was no longer struggling. He released his fingers from the dirty mat of hair and climbed slowly to his feet. With a hand that shook a good deal he wiped the blood from his eyes then went to Manders' horse and took the canteen from the saddle. He drank thirstily then tilting his head back allowed some of the water to flow over his face and head. He used the sleeve of his shirt to mop away the excess water then went and stood over Manders. As far as he could see, the man had not moved. He stood watching for a long time then slowly turned away and climbed on to the sorry beast that had borne him all day.

He supposed he was a murderer and one day sooner or later he would hang. Taking the horse was a hanging matter too, but he felt too utterly weary to bother about it. In any case, he could only hang once.

He went three or four miles in the fast deepening darkness before it occurred to him that he was intolerably hungry and might just as well have brought some food along with him. Manders would have no need of it now. Johnny would have turned back but he was doubtful of finding his way. Or was it that he was afraid to go where there lay a dead man? The thought was of such importance to him that he reined in the horse to sort the matter out. After a few seconds he felt a peculiar sense of elation.

He wasn't afraid of the dead man. He was certain of that. Neither did he fear being hanged. In fact he didn't know anything that he was really afraid of. He spent quite a few minutes savouring the totally new feeling, then a deadly tiredness crept over him. He eased himself from the saddle, unbuckled the cinch, and careless of whether the horse wandered or not, threw himself on the ground using the saddle for a pillow.

Three days later, having followed the course of the San Juan river he came to Cartersville. He had heard of the place but knew little of it except that it was near to where his parents' home had once been. The town took its name from Luke Carter, owner of the Silver Dollar saloon, and reckoned itself to be a law-abiding, but free and easy place, depending for its existence on the neighbouring cattle ranches, of which Mark Donovan's hundred thousand acre spread over-shadowed all others.

Johnnie let his horse bring itself to a halt and gazed around in some wonder. In the years he had worked for Manders, the sheepherder had not once allowed him to come near a town. The place awed him. Twenty or thirty people, a few of them women, moved about in the street and just ahead of where he had halted, half a dozen men lounged on a veranda. Johnnie had just finished spelling out the name over the veranda, *Carter's Silver Dollar Saloon*, when a tall angular looking man heaved himself from a chair and walked towards him. Johnnie caught the glint of the star on the man's shirt and muttered to himself.

'Well, it's bound to be sooner or later. Might as well be now. I sure hope I get a chance to see over the place first, though.'

Then the marshal was standing in front of him, taking in everything from the shock of corn coloured hair above the thin, sun-scorched face to the ragged shirt and jeans and the split and scuffed up boots.

'Where're you from, sonny, and what do they call you?'

'Johnnie, Johnnie Callum – I worked with a sheepie, back there,' he gestured vaguely over his shoulder. 'I quit him

10

three days since. I—'

It was in Johnnie's mind to say, 'I killed him,' but he decided to keep his newly found freedom as long as he could.

'Worked with a sheepie, eh? What was his name?'

'Josh Manders.' Johnnie blurted out the name defiantly and waited for the marshal's hand to move towards his gun, but he only said in a disinterested tone:

'Manders? Yeah – I reckon I've heard of him some place. What are you going to do next, sonny? We don't have any sheep around this place. In fact we wouldn't tolerate the stinking beasts.'

A smile lit Johnnie's face. So the marshal didn't know Manders was dead. He could hang on to his freedom for a while yet.

'I'll get other work,' he said confidently.

'Yeah? What at? There's only range work in these parts and you're no range hand, by the looks of you. I reckon you'd best move on, young feller.'

Johnnie nodded, unabashed by the order to leave town: 'If I could just water the horse, Marshal, and fill my canteen.'

'There's a pump and a trough just a little ways up the street.'

Marshal Hennesey turned away and walked back to the saloon veranda. He hadn't particularly liked doing what he had just done. On the other hand he was not over worried about it. Carter, who paid his salary, expected him to keep the town clear of loafers and no-goods and to his mind, Johnnie fitted into one of the categories. As he stepped on to the veranda again, Judge Bohun took his cigar from his fat lips and said idly:

'What's the score, Ed?'

Hennesey flopped down in his chair: 'Young feller, calls himself Johnnie Callum, reckons he's quit working with a

11

sheepie name Manders. I told him to move on. Feller looks like he's about half starved. My gosh, it's hot this afternoon.'

Bohun shifted his bulk, brushed cigar ash from his brocade waistcoat and agreed that it was hot.

Carlen, who ran the drygoods store in between bouts of sitting on the veranda of the Silver Dollar, got to his feet, yawned and stretched his stringy frame: 'I reckon I'd best be going, gents. It don't do to let an assistant be too long by hisself in the store business. Some of them gets funny ideas about what belongs to them.'

The others grunted assent and watched him walk the length of the dusty street then stop within a few feet of Johnnie.

'Ed says he's chased you out of town,' Carlen began conversationally, at the same time running a professional eye over Johnnie's ragged clothing.

'Ed?'

'Yeah, Ed Hennesey, the marshal.'

'He told me I'd best move on.'

'Amounts to the same thing.' Carlen squirted tobacco juice then ranged his eyes over Johnnie's shoulder to a rig that was entering the far end of the street. 'If you had some new clothes you might find yourself a job and be able to stay.'

Johnnie smiled ingenuously: 'I'd need money for new clothes and if I had that I reckon I'd spend it on a meal.'

Carlen continued to stare at the rig until he was certain it was that belonging to Sam Stevens and his sister Lucy, then he came to a decision.

'I could mebbe fix you with a job and clothes and a meal. The job won't pay much, mind you, an' you'll have to work almighty hard. I guess you'd owe me most of your first month's pay. Would you do a deal like that?'

Johnnie hesitated. Not at the idea of handing over a month's pay but with the thought in his mind that if he was arrested and hanged he would not be able to pay back the loan. Finally, he decided that since he had committed murder and stolen a horse, paying back a loan would hardly matter.

'I'd be real glad to make the deal,' he smiled.

'Then come on down to my store. That's Sam Stevens just pulling up with that rig. Sam's a great friend of mine and he'll give you a job if I ask him. You let me do the talking, though. Sam ain't the kind that listens to just anyone.'

Johnnie nodded and, as Carlen hurried towards the store, trailed after him leading the horse. He stopped a few yards from the rig, saw Carlen engage Sam Stevens in conversation, then fixed wondering eyes on the girl.

Never had he seen or dreamt of any creature half so beautiful. He had no words to describe to himself the soft cloud of dark hair that framed and set off the browned, demure face, neither could he have assessed in words the trim figure seated so gracefully on the hard seat of the rig, but he knew it was all breath-takingly lovely.

The girl became conscious of his stare and gave a sudden shift of her head that made Johnnie gaze self-consciously at his boots, then Carlen called him over. Carlen made a heavy-handed introduction, then Johnnie stood silent while Sam Stevens appraised him with keen blue eyes.

'Is that right?' Stevens asked, 'you're willing to work for us for ten dollars a month?'

'That's right, Mr Stevens.'

'It's not much pay but it's all we can afford. By the time you get some clothes from Mr Carlen here, you'll have very little left.'

'It'll be more than I've ever had before.'

Stevens stared at him for a moment then fished in his back pocket and brought out a slim roll of bills. He peeled off ten dollars and handed them to Carlen.

'See that he gets value,' he said briefly.

'I'll take him over to Joe's place.'

As Carlen moved away taking Johnnie with him, Lucy got down from the wagon and stood her five feet two inches square in front of her brother's six-feet-one: 'That was a fine, smart thing to do, Sam.'

He looked at her good humouredly: 'What was, Luce?'

'You know very well what I'm talking about. Taking on that boy for ten dollars a month when he could hire out anywhere for thirty. I'm ashamed that you should do such a thing.'

Sam pushed back his Stetson and scratched at his stubborn red hair: 'Didn't altogether cotton to the notion myself, Luce, but the kid seems to be pretty near starving and in need of a job mighty quick. And of course it's all right you saying he could earn thirty a month. The fact is he couldn't. Who else but us would hire a sheepie and I did tell him it was all we could afford.'

'Well, I think it's terrible, and that Mr Carlen will swindle him every way he can.'

'Well, whichever way it is, the kid's better off than he was ten minutes ago. At least he'll have a meal and clothes and more meals to come. Now suppose you 'tend to what stores we want while I go along and see Carter about that loan?'

Lucy smiled: 'All right, sorry for blowing my top.'

She was still in the store when Carlen came in with Johnnie and affected to take little notice when the pair went to the far end of the long counter and Carlen began throwing jeans and shirts in front of Johnnie. However, she was forced to take notice ten minutes later when Johnnie came out of some back part of the store dressed in a new outfit and walked straight to her.

'Be all right if I carry these things out to the rig, ma'am?' Johnnie indicated the growing pile of stores on the counter.

'Yes, I guess it will, Johnnie.'

She watched discreetly as he handled heavy packages and bags with a certain amount of awkwardness but with undoubted strength. He was a boy yet, she decided, with all her seventeen years of woman's wisdom, but with a few months of real feeding and range work he would be man enough.

Stevens came back by the time the rig was loaded, a frown on his usually sunny face. He helped his sister to the seat of the rig then climbed up himself and took the reins. As they moved off with Johnnie riding behind them she asked the question to which she already knew the answer:

'Did you get it, Sam?'

'Not a dime. I practically got down on my knees to Carter, blast him, but I reckon he's scared of Donovan. Wouldn't say, of course, but he kept hinting that the best way out of our troubles was to sell to Donovan.'

'Damn Donovan,' the girl muttered, then aloud, 'Why should he want our tiny spread, a thousand acres against his hundreds of thousands?'

'He could do with our water,' Sam said morosely.

'Yes, the water father fought for and against Donovan, too. I tell you, Sam, I'd shoot it out with Donovan before I'd let him have an inch of our land.'

'You forget we have law now, Luce.'

'Yes, Carter's law and he's scared of Donovan. Oh, for a man big enough to clean up on him.'

'Well, I don't reckon to be a coward, Luce, but cleaning Donovan up means taking on a whole bunch of gunslingers at the same time.'

'Oh, I didn't mean it that way, Sam, you're brave enough for anything, but I feel as if there ought to be someone big enough for Donovan and his gunslingers too.'

'Johnnie Callum maybe,' Sam laughed.

'Johnnie Callum,' Lucy repeated. 'Yes, some day,

15

Johnnie's going to be a very big man. Perhaps big enough for Donovan.'

'Ah, now, Luce, quit kidding.'

'But I'm not kidding.'

CHAPTER TWO

In his office at the back of the Silver Dollar Carter sat moodily in front of his desk. A whiskey bottle and a part emptied glass was near his hand and the smoke from a long cigar curled upwards from an ashtray. The ashtray was silver, like the lamp that stood close to it. The desk was mahogany, so was the chair Carter sat on. The remaining furniture, four easy chairs, a side table and a couch were of the same richly coloured wood and stood on a thickly piled carpet. Mirrors in gilt frames covered a large area of the walls and a final tribute to Carter's wealth was a small iron safe in one corner of the room.

Carter barely lifted his head as the room door opened and a woman entered, though the entry of Belle Clancy into a room was sufficient to make most men turn and stare. With a head of honey coloured hair dressed in small tight curls, a generous exposure of a creamy neck and bosom and a good figure moulded in wine coloured velvet, Belle carried her forty years with ease and grace. And if powder and paint did cover a few age lines on her face, the green eyes were still youthful and the mouth full and rich. A man would have to be very keen to see that about both eyes and mouth was a certain hardness.

Belle gave a glance at Carter: 'Worrying about Donovan again?'

'In a way, Belle.' Carter stood up, a tall, thin man with a wispy black moustache pomaded to pointed ends. He straightened his frock-coat, smoothed down the black waistcoat and satisfied himself by a glance at one of the mirrors that his black, waved hair was still tidy.

'In a way,' she said half mockingly. 'Don't tell your partner anything right away, will you? Make me guess like I've always had to do.'

Something of a smile came to Carter's face. 'Well, you usually guess rightly, Belle.'

Swiftly the amusement in her eyes faded. 'Usually – yes.'

'Now, Belle. You don't have to keep on remembering.'

'Don't have to? No, I don't have to, but how the hell can I ever forget? Eight years and it's as clear as yesterday. You and me riding high and handsome. The saloon doing well. Then Donovan came in the place and got into the poker game you were running. If only he'd quit when the running was against him like the others did. But no, he has to finish it out with you in the office, me serving the pair of you drinks.'

'Stop it, Belle,' Carter snapped. 'You're getting hysterical. Donovan took a mighty big chance when he put all he had against the saloon.'

Belle fought down her hysteria. 'Sure, he was a good gambler, I'll give the devil that much. But I had a stupid hunch that he was bluffing. If I hadn't given you the nod you could have refused his raise and let him get away with a few thousand dollars. You would have refused that raise, wouldn't you? His ranch against the saloon?'

'I don't know, Belle. Maybe I would, maybe I wouldn't. Anyway, it's done with now. Let's forget it.'

She nodded. 'All right, pour me a drink, and I'll try to forget that I made you Donovan's man of work and that you

18

dare hardly breathe without consulting him. Now tell me what it was that worried you before I started.'

'Sam Stevens came in to see me about a loan, and of course I had to refuse him. Donovan would have been down on me like a herd of stampeding bulls if I'd helped Sam out.'

'Poor Sam. Lucy too, I guess. It's going to hurt them like hell when Donovan does finally squeeze them out.'

'I wouldn't have felt so bad about it if Sam's father hadn't been a friend of mine.'

'Well, we've troubles enough of our own, I reckon. Those two are young and strong, maybe they'll make out. Anyway, it's time we showed in the saloon, things'll be starting to brisk up, and who knows? Donovan might give us a visit. He's not been near for almost a month.'

Carter nodded and held the door open for her to pass in front of him. He passed a quick eye over the large room and saw that the place was moderately full. Two poker games were in progress from which the house would take ten per cent, and a dozen or more men were already drinking at the bar. All very satisfactory, Carter thought bitterly, except that three-quarters of the profits went to Donovan. He moved to the bar and one of the two bartenders poured him a whiskey from his own special bottle. Belle, he noticed, had gone straight to one of the poker games and was watching the play intently. It was one of her favourite occupations and had been one of his own at one time. Now he never glanced at a card, let alone touched one. The game with Donovan had been his last.

Hennesey pushed through the batwings and held them open for Judge Bohun, and the pair came and stood by Carter.

'On me,' Bohun puffed. 'Whiskey for both of you gents?'

Both men nodded and the bartender set up the drinks.

'We had a stranger in town this afternoon,' the judge told

Carter. 'Didn't stay long though. Ed here told him to be on his way and the kid was just moving when Sam Stevens came in. As far as we could see from the veranda Sam gave the kid a job. He got some new clothes from the store as well,' Bohun chuckled. 'We all reckon Carlen fixed that and took a good rake off the kid's pay.'

'Kid?' Carter questioned idly.

'Yeah, a fair haired youngster, about eighteen, I guess,' Hennesey put in. 'Said his name was Callum. Been workin' for a sheepie.'

'Callum,' Carter said sharply.

'That's right, Johnnie Callum. Why, have you heard the name before?'

'I heard there were some homesteaders of that name way out on Donovan's range. That'd be about six or seven years back.'

'Sure, there was a whole bunch of families squatted about thirty miles east of Sam Stevens's spread,' Bohun said. 'Donovan cleared the lot out. That'd be a couple of years before your time, Ed.'

'Before we had any kind of law,' Carter said. He leaned towards the bartender. 'Better light the lamps, Morgan. Those fellows won't be able to see their cards soon.'

Bohun drained his glass: 'I reckon I'll sit down, gents, my feet are killing me. How about a hand of cards, Marshal, just to pass the time?'

'Not me, Judge, here's your man now, coming through the batwings.'

Bohun turned his head and glimpsed the figure of Donovan. 'Too high for me,' he muttered as he shuffled away from the bar.

Donovan entered with Stone, his top-hand, treading close behind him. A big man in every way, Donovan topped everyone else in the room and his great width of shoulder made the other men seem puny by comparison. The voice too was big, and boomed as he called out:

'Hello, Judge, where are you scuttling to? Come on up to the counter, man. Hello, Marshal, Carter and the rest of you. Morgan, set them up five, no, six. Hell, I nearly forgot you, Belle.'

Belle turned slowly from the poker game she was watching, gave Donovan a cool stare, then said:

'I'll have mine over here. Gin if you don't mind.'

'Just as you like, Belle, though if you were a man I'd make you step up to the bar lively enough, like the judge here.'

'But I'm not, so you can't.' There was a sharpness in her voice that made Donovan stare for a moment, then he turned to Carter.

'Something bitten her?' he demanded loudly. 'If so, you'd better keep her under control.'

Carter whitened but made no reply.

'I'm talking to you,' Donovan boomed. 'You heard what I said. Keep her under control.'

Belle walked to the counter, a seductive, swaying cat-like walk: 'You're discussing me, Mr Donovan and making it so the whole saloon can hear. I don't like that.'

Carter put in a 'Now, Belle—' and was cut short by Donovan's bull-like: 'What the hell if I am discussing you? Who's to stop me?'

'No one,' Belle said coolly. 'There's no one to shut you up, Mr Donovan, and there's no one to shut me up either. I can say what I like to you and you can't do a thing about it. You're a loud-mouthed range bully with less manners than any one of your steers. I'll drink your gin because I don't give a hoot who pays for liquor. So remember that next time you call me to the counter.'

She drank the gin in one gulp and walked back to the poker game.

21

Donovan turned a brick red then said thickly: 'Carter, I'll have a word with you in your office.'

Without waiting for a reply he strode towards the office. Stone made as if to follow but Donovan barked: 'I can handle this alone. You just see no one interrupts.'

Carter gave a shrug of his shoulders that was significant of something neither the judge nor Hennesey could understand, then followed Donovan into the office.

'I guess I'll take a walk,' Bohun said to Hennesey as Stone planted himself with his back to the office door.

Hennesey's gaze was directed at Belle whose eyes were fixed either on the closed door of the office or else on the hard jawed, thin lipped face of Stone in front of it.

'Yeah, Judge. You do that. Keep right out of any trouble.' Hennesey's voice was full of sarcasm.

Bohun rolled his bulk towards the batwings, making the only movement in the now silent room. A few eyes watched his crossing of the floor but most were directed either at Stone or Belle.

Belle fingered the locket she wore at the end of a long gold chain, then moved towards the office door, the velvet of her skirts making a soft swishing. She stopped within a foot of Stone then said softly:

'You're in my way, Stone.'

'Donovan doesn't want to be interrupted.' Stone did not look at her as he spoke but kept his gaze fixed on Hennesey, who with his back to the bar, had a significantly clear space to each side of him.

Belle turned her head: 'Marshal, I want to go into the office. I'm Carter's partner and have a perfect right to go in and out when I choose.'

'You'd better stand aside, Stone, and let the lady do what she wants,' Hennesey said quietly.

Stone's right hand lifted and the fingers hovered over the

butt of his gun. Then he relaxed.

'OK, Marshal. Have it your own way. Donovan said we weren't to buck the law. Maybe he'll change his mind some day.'

He turned quickly and flung the office door open: 'The Marshal says I've got to let her in, boss.'

The words were flung past Belle as she walked into the room and closed the door behind her.

Donovan's face was choleric: 'So you figure to buck me, Belle? Well, you know what happens to people that do that?'

'Pretty well, Mr Donovan. Some gets hounded off their land, a few get killed, but in any case there's a raw deal coming to them. Just what kind of a hand do you figure to serve me?'

'He wants to drive you out of town,' Carter said thickly. 'I've told him that if you go, I go as well.'

'Which doesn't suit Mr Donovan at all. Does it, Donovan? No, you're all right as a range bully. A sort of Emperor, but when it comes to keeping a town going, even a small town, you don't measure up. And you need this town, don't you? Need it for its stores and its freight line and its saloon to keep your boys happy when they're tired of stamping round your mighty empire. Well, I'm just plain tired of seeing all the dollars going in your direction and I'm pulling out on the morning coach. Carter can come with me or stay and slave for you. Whichever he pleases.'

'And a hell of a way you'll get on your own,' Donovan sneered. 'Do you suppose for a minute that Carter'll go with you? No damn fear, he's got it soft here and he—'

'I'll be with Belle, wherever she goes,' Carter said in a tired voice.

Donovan moved towards the door: 'Then the more fool you, if you want to starve with her.'

He had his hand on the knob of the door when Belle said,

in an entirely different voice:

'Mr Donovan. I don't think I'd like the idea of starving. Just what have I to do to please you?'

Donovan turned and stared at her, seeing a light in her eyes that he had never before noticed. It came to him, that with the light of the lamp turning her bare arms and shoulders to a delicate cream, she was a very desirable woman.

'Just keep the sting out of that tongue of yours,' he said gruffly.

'I could try, but a woman feels a lack of money and things more than a man does. This dress for instance. I've had it more than four years. Maybe it looks all right to you but—'

Carter stared at her with unbelieving eyes. Belle, playing the traitress after all the years they had been together. Yet there was no misreading the look of invitation she was giving to Donovan or the lascivious acceptance in his hard, grey eyes. Carter's hand fumbled at a drawer in the desk but Donovan saw the move and read its significance.

'If that's a gun you're after, Carter, drop the idea. I could shoot you before you had it half out of the drawer.'

Carter drew away from the desk and stood rigidly. He had made his play, a feeble enough attempt, and failed. Now he could only watch Belle sell him down the river.

Donovan said, as if Carter was no longer in the room: 'Belle, if new dresses and falderals will keep you sweet, then get the darn things.'

Belle did the next to impossible, she simpered: 'Now, Mr Donovan, a girl has to keep some pride, you know.'

'Pride, hell! What do you want, woman? Listen, take over the running of the saloon and I'll promise not to poke into the expenses too much.'

'And be a kept woman again like I am now?'

Carter burst forward: 'Belle! Whatever are you saying? You

know we've always split things even, you and I.'

Belle did not even turn her eyes away from Donovan's flushed face and as Carter fell back again, she went on:

'You know, Mr Donovan, I think on the whole I'd rather take a chance on starvation. After all, I'm not bad looking and pretty women are not exactly ten a penny in the West. You got this place by a gamble which would have left you pretty poor if you'd lost. I think perhaps I'll take a gamble on my looks. Yes, I'll take the morning stage.' She turned to Carter. 'Sorry the break had to come this way, Luke, but I guess it had to be. Maybe we'll do better apart.'

Carter started to say something but Donovan got in first: 'Belle, you say you'll take a gamble. How about having one with me? The saloon against yourself?'

Belle's blue eyes filled with caution. 'Now wait a minute, those stakes need explaining.'

Donovan came towards her and took hold of her arms, holding her so that she was forced to look into his burning eyes: 'I'll stake the saloon and everything that's in it against yourself. If you lose, you run this place and the town for me as I want it run. Do I have to make things any clearer?'

Belle laughed, a high-pitched, brittle laugh that set Carter's spine crawling. She stopped laughing suddenly and said:

'You've got yourself a bet, Mister. I'll take it on the cut of the cards and before witnesses. The judge and the marshal.'

Hot colour mounted in Donovan's face as he released her. 'Don't trust my word, eh? Well, you shall have your witnesses.' He turned and wrenched open the door. 'Stone, find that so-called judge and have him and Hennesey come in here.'

'Judge has just come in again,' Stone said. 'Reckon he couldn't keep his nose out of anything for long.' He bawled across the saloon. 'Hey, Judge, and you as well, Hennesey, the boss wants you.'

The pair came into the office, Bohun puffing at a cigar to cover his nervousness. Hennesey, cool and collected but apprehensive of more trouble than he would be able to handle. His eyes went first to Donovan's broad face and saw the red flush that extended from the man's bull neck to his iron grey hair. Donovan, he decided, was at bursting point but whether it was anger or some other emotion that moved the man, it did not show. Carter was easily assessed if one could think of a dead man as standing upright. Belle, on the other hand, was exuberant, apparently filled with a triumph and finding it hard not to make a great display of it. It took a couple of minutes to explain the gamble and to draw up two documents, one of which would give Belle the ownership of the saloon whilst the other bound her to work for Donovan until he was pleased to release her.

Bohum, now that there seemed no danger to himself, took the cigar from his mouth: 'A mighty fine gamble, I should say. Yes, sir, one that will go down in history.'

He gave a cackling laugh which Hennesey cut short with: 'Shut up, Bohun. Belle, are you sure you're making this gamble of your own free will?'

'And what if she isn't? Donovan demanded.

Hennesey's hand moved a little nearer his gun: 'I'm asking Belle,' he said quietly.

'Don't worry about me, Ed. Just stand by to see me win the gamble of my life.'

She turned so quickly that her heavy skirts swirled about her and darting to the side table wrenched open a drawer. 'Here you are, Mr Donovan, a dozen new packs. Pick where you like.'

Donovan moved towards the table. 'Sure nice new packs. Where shall I pick, from the top or the bottom?'

He took so long in making his choice that the others, with the exception of Carter, crowded round him. He seemed suddenly to find life in his limbs and with one quick move reached his desk, yanked open a drawer and whipped out a .45 Colt.

Hennesey was the first to turn to the sound and find himself looking at the muzzle of the gun and as the others faced about, Carter spoke thickly.

'Stand away from Donovan, all of you. I'm going to let the bastard have what he deserves.'

Bohun moved hastily to one side but neither Belle or Hennesey stirred.

Carter waved the gun: 'Hennesey, you're in the line of fire.'

'Stand out of the way,' Donovan boomed. 'Whatever's coming I want a chance to draw.'

Hennesey made a reluctant side step: 'It'll be murder if you pull that trigger, Luke.'

'Is that so? Well, you're going to be a first class witness.' Carter's thumb hooked over the hammer of the weapon, then Belle's voice came shrilly.

'Are you going to cheat me of the only decent chance I've had in years?'

'Cheat you, Belle? You know I wouldn't do that.'

'Then lower that gun and let me have my chance.'

Carter tossed the gun on the desk: 'If you want it that way, Belle. I thought perhaps – but never mind.'

Donovan made a sharp intake of breath and ripped the cover from the pack that was in his hand: 'These will do. Let's get it over. You can have the first cut if you like, Belle.'

She shook her head: 'I want no favours. You cut first.'

Donovan lifted nearly half of the pack and showed a queen of hearts. 'I clean forgot to make a shuffle,' he said. 'Shall I do it again?'

Belle smiled. 'You've had your cut, now I'll take mine.' She reached firm fingers towards the pack. 'Don't go too heavy for the omen stuff, Donovan. You're likely to be disappointed like this.'

She lifted a dozen or so cards and displayed the ace of clubs.

Donovan gave her a glare of complete hatred and then burst from the room. Belle stood for a moment, the cards still in her hands, then unexpectedly, as far as the men watching her were concerned, she gave a little sigh and slumped to the floor.

Both Carter and Hennesey ran to raise her to her feet, and as they lifted her on to the settee, Judge Bohun boomed out:

'By the lord! Belle Clancy throwing a faint. I'll believe anything after that.'

In a few seconds, Belle stirred, then sat upright, her eyes going immediately to the judge. 'That paper Donovan signed, it's legal enough.'

'They don't make them any more legal,' Bohun said. 'Lord, Belle, I never thought I'd see the day when anyone would get the best of Donovan.'

Hennesey put his hand on the knob of the door. 'I guess Belle could do with resting up a little. Judge.'

'Sure, sure. I reckon I can take a hint, Marshal.'

As the door closed behind the pair, Carter reached for the pack of cards that had decided the bet. He shuffled and cut several times and on each occasion turned up an ace. He looked at Belle.

'Convex aces. So there wasn't any gamble.'

'Pour me a drink, Luke. I feel like I've been in the middle of a stampede. There was a little gamble but not much. I've noticed that Donovan sometimes spreads that big hand of his across the length of the pack when he takes a cut.'

Carter handed her a glass of whiskey. 'Suppose he'd done it this time and perhaps lifted the ace of spades? Belle, you took a hell of a risk.'

She gulped down her drink. 'I had to. Ever since the day you lost this place to Donovan I've had those packs of cards waiting for him.' She got to her feet and gave a slightly hysterical laugh. 'You nearly spoiled the whole thing when you dragged that gun out of the drawer. But I'm glad you had a try, Luke. Yes, I'm darned glad you had a try.'

'Almost wish I'd succeeded,' Carter said moodily.

'What, and have Hennesey hang you for murder?'

'It would have been that way, Belle, if you'd lost the gamble. I'd have got Donovan some way rather than let him have you.'

Belle gripped his arm tightly. 'We've got the saloon back and that's all that matters and we'll go places together like we've always done. Now, I'm going to show up in the saloon. Suppose you put those packs of cards into the stove and burn them? Every last one of them.'

CHAPTER THREE

Two months with Sam and Lucy put much needed flesh on to Johnnie's bony frame. He acquired, clumsily at first but with increasing dexterity, some skill in rounding up stray cattle and in the running down and roping of unbranded calves. He worked willingly from sunup to sundown and at the end of the day slept alone in the bunkhouse that had been built to hold a dozen men. He was entirely content with his life and had no yearnings or ambitions. Or at least, it was that way with him for most of the time. There were other times, brief and fleeting, when he thought of Josh Manders and the way he had left him. Then, he had the beginnings of a fear. The fear that this contentment, this period of regular eating, sleeping and working, would be snatched away from him by the arrival of the marshal to arrest him for the killing of Manders. There were times, too, when either Sam or Lucy spoke to him that he wondered if he shouldn't tell them that they harboured a killer. The feeling came to him mostly when he was talking to Lucy. She, somehow, had the capacity of making it seem to him that her clear, brown eyes looked right into his thoughts.

She had him feeling that way this morning when she said:

'Johnnie, harness the light rig, will you? Then you can drive me into town. Sam isn't going this time, he wants to finish some accounts.'

Johnnie said: 'Yes, ma'am,' and was about to move towards the barn when Lucy said:

'Just a minute, Johnnie. I've your pay here, or don't you want it?' Her brown eyes smiled at him.

'Pay! No, I guess I don't need it, ma'am. I've got shirts and jeans and such. Maybe you wouldn't mind saving it until I get around to needing it?'

'What! No drink at the end of the month? No tobacco and papers? Johnnie, you do live hard.'

Johnnie grinned. 'I reckon it's kinda soft living, ma'am. Besides, I ain't used to drinking and smoking.' He paused then went on seriously. 'Perhaps I ought to learn to smoke, though. Most grown men does it.'

Lucy turned away. 'You'll be man enough one day, Johnnie, without either drinking or smoking.'

Puzzled as to her meaning, Johnnie went to the barn, dragged out the light rig and put a pair of horses to it. Still pondering her last remark, he drove towards town without speaking. Three miles of the rutted trail were covered when a little cloud of dust showed a rider coming towards them. Johnnie put the rig over to the right-hand side of the trail to give the approaching rider room to pass, then at a word from Lucy reined the team to a halt.

The rider drew alongside of them and his gaze went enquiringly to Johnnie at the same time as he said:

'Morning, Lucy. I was on my way to your place.'

'Morning, Stone. Is it anything I can do or do you have to see Sam—'

'Not particularly. I've got a message for Sam from the boss. I guess you could tell it to your brother when you get back. This the kid I heard you'd hired?'

'This is Johnnie Callum and he's hired to us. What's Mr Donovan's message?'

31

'Just that Sam should come into town tonight to see him. He wants to talk to him some.'

'Well, Sam's mighty busy right now. Can't Mr Donovan ride this way himself?'

Stone grinned. 'Perhaps I put the message the wrong way. It's for Sam to come and see Donovan. Kind of an order.'

'We don't take orders from Mr Donovan or anyone else,' Lucy said sharply. 'You tell him that when you get back. You can also say that he's welcome to call on us at any time, but if he wants to talk about buying our place, that's definitely out.'

'Maybe he'll take it when he gets around to thinking that way,' Stone jeered.

'Maybe he'll try and if he does I expect you'll be amongst those gunning for him.'

Stone looked at her for a moment, then a suggestive leer came into his eyes. 'Depends on yourself. For instance if you were to be sort of nice to me—'

He got that far when Lucy made a quick snatch at the long whip that lay near her feet. She had it raised when Stone made a long reach from the saddle and grabbed her by the arm. The quickness of the two moves found Johnnie temporarily bereft of movement. He had not fully understood the gist of the conversation between Lucy and Stone although he had gathered that there was some kind of difference between them. Also, the mention of Donovan's name had brought about an emotion that he could not explain. His moment of inaction was short, in fact just long enough for Stone to twist the whip from Lucy's grasp. Then, Johnnie left the seat of the rig in a spring that carried him clear across Lucy and whirled Stone from his saddle. The pair hit the ground solidly with the foreman underneath. He was partly winded but otherwise unhurt and for the moment, surprised more than angered at being attacked by one he regarded as a kid. Anger came a second later when the kid's hands fastened in his hair and thumped his head sickeningly against the ground. In a moment he had kneed Johnnie in the groin and as the hold in his hair broke, twisted himself uppermost and came quickly to his feet. He did not wait for Johnnie to rise but immediately drove a boot at his ribs. Unskilled at fighting, Johnnie took the full force of the kick and only reached out blindly as Stone kicked again. He got a hold on the foreman's boot, tried to throw the man and when he did not succeed, hung on desperately. He heard Lucy scream something and for some reason lifted his eyes towards Stone's. The foreman, fighting to hold his balance, was dragging his sixgun from its holster. Johnnie saw death coming to him and moved with the speed of a frightened animal. He let go his hold on Stone's boot, came up to a crouch and seized the foreman's gunhand in both his own. He gave a wrench to the wrist that sent the gun whirling. Stone screeched with pain and brought his knee against Johnnie's chin. Johnnie went sprawling. He should have been unconscious from such a blow, and in fact saw two of the foreman as he staggered to his feet. Head down, eyes almost closed, he rushed at Stone again. This time the foreman dealt a left-handed punch to the jaw that sent him floundering against the horses. He rebounded senselessly and bored in again. Stone, surprised by the quick return to the attack, got the full impact of Johnnie's blond head somewhere about his chin. He went down flat and an avalanche of arms and legs seemed to fling at him. Next, his head was bounced against the ground, twice in rapid succession. It was more than even a tough foreman could stand, and Stone felt his senses slipping. Johnnie, on the other hand, felt nothing at all. He saw Stone's face through a red blur and desired nothing but to kill the man. He slammed the foreman's head downwards a third and fourth time before he felt the hands tugging at his shoulder and the voice imploring him to stop. Then suddenly the blur vanished and he saw Stone's face clearly again. The face of an apparently dead man. He got to his feet slowly and became aware that it was Lucy who had been tugging at his shoulder and yelling for him to let up. He looked at her, his mind filled with the conviction that he had killed Stone and now there could be no escaping the law. He expected to see either anger or repugnance in her eyes, but instead they glinted with something very like glee.

'You don't have to half kill every man who insults me,' she said.

'You mean he ain't dead? Look at him, he ain't stirring.'

'You look at him. Can't you see the rise and fall of his chest? Get the canteen from the wagon, you'll soon see how much alive he is. No, wait a minute. Pick his gun up and unload it.'

Johnnie stooped and picked up the weapon. He handled it so badly that Lucy shouted:

'For land's sake put it down again. You'll kill one of us.'

Johnnie dropped the weapon hastily. 'I ain't ever—' he began, but Lucy stopped him.

'I can see you haven't. We'll attend to that as soon as maybe. Meantime, I'll see to it.'

She picked up the gun and rapidly ejected the shells. 'There, that'll give Mr Stone time to cool off if he feels like blasting at you. Now pour some water over him.'

Johnnie removed the stopper from the canteen and allowed water to trickle over the foreman's face. In a second or two, Stone began to splutter and gasp, then he sat up with a jerk. It was a moment before full comprehension returned, but as soon as it did he placed both hands on the ground with the intention of heaving himself to his feet. He gave the heave and then a howl of pain as his right wrist crumpled under his weight.

Johnnie looked at him in some surprise. 'Seems like you've busted that wrist, Mr Stone.'

Stone got up with difficulty. '*I've busted it*! Why, you young cub, you did that when you ripped my gun out of my hand.'

He picked up the gun that Lucy had thrown down again, and left-handedly thumbed back the hammer. 'I've half a notion to drill you full of holes, you young snake-in-the grass, but as it is I'll let you live and run you out of the country. Ever been run out of a place afore? You runs in front of my hoss, see? An' if you start to lag I quicken you up with a slug as near to your boots as I can manage. Go on, get movin'.' He waved the six-gun at Johnnie. 'Go on, before I try a shot at your toes.'

'I wouldn't do that if I were you, Stone,' Lucy said.

'Oh, and why not?'

'Because I took the precaution of pulling the shells from your gun and because Johnnie, who handled you when you had two hands and a gun, can certainly manage you now you're one-handed. I suggest you climb on your horse and go back to your boss. Give him my answer, which is also Sam's answer, and explain to him how you got your wrist broken.'

Johnnie braced himself to his full height which was close to six feet. 'There's your horse, Mister, and you heard what the lady said. Now get riding.'

Stone went towards his mount. 'I'll meet you again, you young fool, and next time I'll cut you down to size.'

Johnnie watched him ride off, then climbed with Lucy to the seat of the rig. He gave an involuntary grunt of pain as he reached for the reins. Lucy glanced at him with some concern.

'Does it hurt badly, Johnnie?'

'No, ma'am. At least not more than when Josh Manders used to belt me around.'

'Josh Manders! Oh, yes, I remember, he was the sheepie

you used to work for. How long were you with him?'

'About six years, near as I know.' Johnnie slapped the reins across the horses' rumps. 'Giddap, come on. We ain't got all day.'

Lucy detected a note of rising anger in the words shouted at the team and wondered what hidden, raw spot her question had probed. She said quietly:

'It sounds as if they were six bad years. Would you like to tell me about them?'

'No, ma'am. I would not.' There was such snap and emphasis in the answer that Lucy coloured. For a jogging mile or so she kept silent, but her eyes went continually to Johnnie's face. The half smile she had become accustomed to seeing had vanished and it was obvious from the heaviness of his expression that Johnnie was deep in troubled thoughts. She tried to think of something to say that would erase the frown, an apology perhaps, but there didn't seem anything to apologise for, at least, no way of putting it into words. Besides, there was now such a firm set to the jaw and mouth that she realized she had now a grown man to deal with and probably an obstinate one at that. It was Johnnie who broke the silence with:

'Ma'am, would it make a lot of trouble for you if I quit when we reach town? I mean after I've loaded the rig with whatever you need?'

Lucy measured her reply carefully. 'Johnnie, it's always inconvenient when a hired man quits suddenly, more so when he's the only one you've got, but there isn't anything either Sam or I could do to hold you. We wouldn't try even if there was. We thought you were happy with us although, of course, we do realize that we're paying you a miserably low wage.'

'I was happy, ma'am, and I ain't bothered about wages. It's just that – heck! You're bound to find out sometime, everyone will. Ma'am, that Josh Manders, I killed him.'

Lucy managed to suppress a start of surprise. 'You'd better tell me the rest. Was Manders knocking you around?'

'Yeah, that was the way of it, ma'am. Josh came at me with his belt like he'd done before, only that time I'd had enough and I got him like I got that feller Stone. Just bashed his head against the ground until he didn't move any more. I'd have done that to Stone if you hadn't stopped me. Ma'am, there must be somethin' bad in me. Somethin' that makes me I don't know what I'm doin', so I reckoned I'd best quit you in case I do somethin' else.'

Now that he had begun to talk Johnnie held nothing back, and it needed few questions from Lucy to give her a complete picture of Johnnie's earlier life. One thing only puzzled her. Although Johnnie had made some reference to Donovan as being the man who had probably been responsible for having his parents hounded off the land, he had made the reference without any sign of resentment. It seemed as if his parents were but a shadow in his past, and that only Josh Manders filled his early life. Manders, she thought, had asked for what he got. But in any case the chances of his body being discovered were remote. Further, carrion birds would have been at work by now, and there would be little left to identify the man in the wild hill country where the fight had taken place. The thing was, to curb Johnnie's desire to run. She said:

'Are you afraid to stand trial, Johnnie?'

'No, ma'am. Least, I don't think so. Before I came to work for you and Sam I didn't give a hoot about the thing. Now, well, I guess I was gettin' to like the life.'

Lucy made a decision. If Johnnie thought he was useful to herself and Sam, he would stay.

'Johnnie, it sounds to me as if Manders went down in a fair enough fight, and if the matter does come to trial there's no one to challenge your word. Sam and I need a fighter on our place. Will you stay?'

Johnnie studied for a moment then said solemnly: 'Yes, ma'am. Glad to.'

'And Johnnie—'

'Yes, ma'am?'

'For land's sake stop calling me ma'am. It isn't right for a man's who just rescued a girl from insults. The name is Lucy. Understand, Lucy.'

'Yes, ma'am – er, Lucy.' Johnnie began to whistle, plaintively and with little melody but with evident enjoyment.

Hennesey was the first man they met with in town. He was moving towards his office and stopped as Johnnie drew up outside the store. The marshal's eyes went quickly to the darkening bruises on Johnnie's face then transferred to Lucy.

'Morning, Lucy. Sam not coming in today?'

'He's busy with the books, Ed, so I thought Johnnie could make the trip with me.'

'Been falling off your horse, young feller?' Hennesey grinned at Johnnie.

Johnnie fingered his bruises. 'No, it wasn't that way, Marshal. I—' He stopped and glanced at Lucy.

Hennesey laughed. 'OK, you don't have to tell if you don't want to.'

'There's no reason why he shouldn't tell,' Lucy put in. 'We met with Matt this morning and he was mighty rude to me. Johnnie chopped him down to size.'

'Johnnie handled Stone! Now look, Lucy, that's kind of hard to swallow. Stone's a big, tough man. Donovan wouldn't have him for foreman if he wasn't. In any case I saw him going into the Silver Dollar about a quarter of an hour since.'

Lucy smiled. 'Go and have a closer look at him, Ed. Then ask him if he fell off his horse. Help me down from the rig, will you, Johnnie?'

Hennesey took a fresh look at Johnnie as he hopped to the ground and extended bony hands towards Lucy. He noticed the size of the hands and the thickness of the wrists and his eyebrows lifted a trifle. He turned away.

'See you again, Lucy, Johnnie.'

He walked towards the Silver Dollar. Seeing Stone was important, more so than the small business he had intended to see to in his office. Stone at any time was a trouble maker and if he had suffered injury at the hands of a mere boy would be doubly so. He climbed the three steps to the veranda of the saloon and pushed through the batwings in a thoughtful frame of mind and the moment he did so he knew that trouble was imminent. Stone was leaning heavily on the bar, a whiskey glass in his left hand, and he was swearing steadily, a monotonous repetition of oaths interspersed with threats 'to fix that young tow-head for good'. Doone, the bartender, was backed from the counter as far as the narrow space allowed and the five or six men on the same side as Stone were giving him ample room. Hennesey recalled as he moved towards the counter that it was the end of the month. Stone was the only Donovan man in town at the moment, but by sundown the place would be packed with MD hands. Some of them would think they owed loyalty to their foreman. Hennesey had the feeling that he was straddling a fence as he drew alongside Stone. The town belonged to Carter and it was from him he received his pay, but just how much could the town buck against the weight of Donovan's spread? And it might be like that if he was too heavy handed with the MD foreman. He was at Stone's back when he said:

'Howdy, Matt. Have the next with me.'

Stone came round slowly, his eyes full of sullen rage. 'What the hell for? I've got dough to buy my own liquor, ain't I?'

'Sure, suit yourself, Matt. Just thought you'd like a beer with me.' His eyes went to Stone's right wrist, now tightly bandaged. 'What happened? You take a spill from your horse?'

'No, I didn't. If you want to know I met up with some young pup that was driving for Lucy Stevens. We had a few words and before I knew what he was at, the skunk dragged me from my saddle. I came down heavily on my right hand. That's all, except that I'll tear his head off his shoulders next time I see him.'

'You ought to go somewhere and get that wrist seen to properly. I reckon it needs a doc by rights.'

'Yeah, and where would I find a doc? Do you think I'm going to take a three-day ride to Lees Ferry? Donovan'll fix it for me when he rides in tonight. Anyway, what the hell's it to you?'

Stone turned sullenly, picked up the whiskey bottle, saw that it was empty, and smashed it down to the floor. 'Doone,' he shouted, 'another bottle. Come on, stir yourself.'

'I reckon you've had about enough, Mr Stone, the boss—'

'To hell with Carter, Belle Clancy as well. They couldn't live if it wasn't for Donovan's spread. Remember that, you bald headed old coot, when you talk to a Donovan man.'

Hennesey nodded to the bartender. 'Give him another bottle, Lem.'

Stone swung round. 'Who the blazes are you to say whether I can have another bottle or not?'

Hennesey met his eyes with a cold stare. 'I'm the marshal, and I'd say if you'd had enough liquor. You haven't. At least, not enough to make you as drunk as you're trying to act. Even if you did get licked in a fight that doesn't say you can fling your temper around wherever you like. Drink as much as you like, but behave or, Donovan man or not, you go into the can.'

Hennesey turned on his heel and went out wondering if he had said the right thing. Clamping down on Stone was one thing, but keeping him clamped down would be something entirely different. It was all right threatening to throw Stone into the lockup. The threat might calm him down for a while, but suppose he was forced to carry out that threat and Donovan should decide he wanted his man out again? What then?

Hennesey confessed to himself that he did not know the answer. The only thing he did know was that sooner or later Donovan was going to stretch out his hand and grab what he wanted. Which would he grab at first, the town or Sam Stevens' place with its abundant supply of water? He guessed at it being the Stevens' place first. Grabbing the town by force had a lot of complications behind it. Taking range land was simple if you had enough guns shooting for you and your conscience was suited to the job. Donovan filled the bill in both respects.

CHAPTER FOUR

Donovan entered the saloon at six in the evening and four men, Harper, Dayley, Morris and Savage walked behind him. The four had the one thing in common. The thin lipped, unsmiling faces of professional gun-hawks. Donovan made immediately for the table at which Stone was seated. He sat himself opposite the foreman while his gun-hawks ranged themselves sideways on to the bar. A position that was both suitable for ordering drinks and keeping an eye to the man who paid them. Carter was at a table at the far end of the room in conversation with Smith, the town's carpenter and odd job man, when the five entered. He took one apprehensive glance, then switched his talk quickly from the subject of a new barn at the livery to an urgent request for Smith to go and ask the marshal to step along.

Stone was part drunk and, with the savage pain in his wrist, inclined to be rebellious. He met Donovan's enquiring eye with a surly: 'Stevens won't come.'

'What exactly did he say?' Donovan asked, then noticing that Stone kept his right hand underneath the table. 'What's wrong with your arm?'

The foreman hesitated, found no effective lie that would cover up the incident and growled out the truth.

'Fine goddam foreman you are,' Donovan said. 'Let me have a look at that wrist.'

Stone unwrapped the bandages and displayed his swollen and discoloured wrist. Donovan probed hard fingers at the joint then turned and bellowed:

'Harper, Savage, here a minute. Play you're being hospital nurses,' he said when the two men strolled over. 'Hold Stone by the shoulders.'

As the hands of both men clamped him back in his chair, Stone glanced nervously at Donovan. 'You're not going to—'

'Shut up,' Donovan boomed. 'You're no use to me with a dislocated wrist.'

He grabbed Stone's hand in his huge grip and gave a pull that brought the foreman forward in spite of the two men holding him back. Stone gave a groan and the moment Donovan released his hold, sagged in his chair.

'He'll be all right,' Donovan said to the pair of gun-hawks. 'You can get back to the bar but go easy with the drinks.' He looked at Stone, now shaking his head from side to side as if to bring things into focus again. 'I'll bet that shook some of the liquor out of you. Get that wrist tied up again and try to listen to what I'm saying. That youngster who pulled you from your horse. What did you say his name was?'

'Callum, Boss. Johnnie Callum. Be about eighteen or nineteen. Stands about six feet and has hair that is darned near white.' Stone struggled with one hand and his teeth to knot the bandage on his wrist.

'Callum, hmm. I seem to remember the name. Yes, I've got it. Not that it matters a damn. Stone, you remember about five or six years back when we cleared four or five bunches of homesteaders off the range? One of them was named Callum. Wasn't it him that came whining up to the ranch house about a son being missing?'

'Well, it's a long time back, Boss, but I do remember

43

clearing some jasper away from the house. I guess the name could have been Callum. You figuring this youngster might be the missing son?'

'Perhaps. Anyway, it's no matter. The thing is, do I go ahead and try to buy Stevens out, or now that you've sort of begun a fight with them, carry on with it. We need that land badly, or rather, the river at that point. Blast it, it's the only place in fifty miles where the banks shelve down at an easy angle. The rest of the course is either sheer rock or clay.'

'I'd be for taking some of the boys up there and making a clean job of it,' Stone growled.

'Huh, I might have expected an answer like that from you. You don't see much further than the end of your nose. I was about set to do that until I lost this saloon back to Belle.'

'I don't see—' Stone began.

'You wouldn't. Listen, owning this saloon is as good or better than owning the rest of the town. It's here where most of the money comes. Money pays Hennesey's wages. Get that?'

'But Hennesey wouldn't dare buck against you, Boss. He ain't ever done it yet. Anyhow, couldn't you hire him direct?'

'Hennesey wouldn't work for me. It was all right while I controlled Carter, but not any more,' Donovan said shortly. 'Carter could tell Hennesey to ask for State help if there was any real trouble. That's the way of it now.' Donovan got to his feet. 'You and I will go and talk to Stevens. Tell the boys to trail along behind us.'

Donovan stalked out of the place and almost collided with Hennesey who was coming in. The two exchanged a brief greeting, then Hennesey continued into the saloon. He gave a nod to Stone and the four who were leaving the counter and went straight up to Carter.

'What's doing, Luke? You worried about those four gunslingers of Donovan's?'

Carter nodded. 'I was, Ed, but I see they're on their way. Maybe I'm a mite jittery these days.'

'Maybe you've good reason to be that way. Donovan's made no move since Belle took the saloon from him.'

'No, that's what worries me. This is the first time he's shown up in the place since that night, and he hasn't even stopped for a drink. I tell you, Ed, I don't like it.'

'No more do I. Stone was on his way to see Sam Stevens when he ran into that trouble, or rather made it for himself.'

'Yes, I got some sort of an idea of what happened from Doone. Nothing very clear, but I make out that that young Callum must be a pretty tough kid.'

Neither man had heard the soft-footed approach of Belle. 'What was that about a tough kid?' she said.

Hennesey retailed what he knew and guessed at. She said, without hesitation:

'If Stone was riding out to see Sam Stevens, it was probably to ask Sam to come here and meet Donovan.'

'I don't see how you make that out,' Carter argued.

'Well, if Donovan has taken Stone with him after only a short talk in here, where else would he be likely to go? Luke, I think these Stevens folk are going to be in trouble.'

Hennesey got to his feet. 'I reckon I might take a little ride that way myself. Been quite a time since I had a look at their place.'

'Mind how you go, Ed,' Carter said. 'Remember what I told you about the Callums being cleared out of their homestead. If this boy is their son he might have some notion about taking vengeance on Donovan.'

'Be a damn good notion if he could manage it,' Belle cut in.

'Seemed a harmless enough youngster when I saw him the first day he came into town,' Hennesey said, 'but after the way he handled Stone, I'm not so sure. Anyway, I guess

45

Donovan can look after himself all right. See you when I get back.'

Donovan had waited a frustrating half hour in front of the Stevens' house when Hennesey rode up. The marshal viewed the big rancher sitting on a cane bottomed chair on the veranda whilst Stone and the other four men lounged against the rail and smoked.

'No one at home,' Hennesey said casually.

'You can see damned well there isn't,' Donovan snapped. 'What brings you here, anyway?'

'Just passing by, thought I'd call in. Like to get around when I can.'

'Hmm, funny day to choose. The end of the month when my boys will be in town raising general hell.'

'Oh, I reckon I'll be back before they get steamed up.' Hennesey slid from his saddle and led his mount to a water trough. He loosed the bit and left the animal drinking while he glanced around. It was easy to see why Donovan coveted this stretch of land, a tightly curved horseshoe of lush grass with the wide loop of the river forming three-quarters of its boundary. The stretch of land was roughly ten miles in either direction and sloped gently down to the river from the rather rough ground at the opening to the horseshoe and it was here that the Stevens' house had been built. Here, also, was the only way out to drive cattle or reach the trail into town. In the days of Sam Stevens' father a wide strip of range from here to the trail had been considered his, but Donovan had slowly pushed the weaker man back until he was contained in the horseshoe and now the only way out was across MD land. Up to now Donovan had never blocked the passage, but Hennesey had often wondered just what would happen if he decided to do so. There seemed to him only two alternatives for Sam. Give in or starve on his own land. Hennesey stared down to the distant loop of the river and followed its gleaming thread. If only there was a break in the cliff-like opposite bank, a place where steers could climb out from the water, Sam could have swam his herd across and driven in that direction. But there was not. Not there or for twelve or so miles in each direction was there any place on the river where cattle could get down to the water. Hennesey put the bit back and was turning the horse away from the trough when he saw three riders silhouetted against the sun. Sam and Lucy Stevens and young Johnnie Callum. The three rode up and put their mounts to the trough. They exchanged greetings with Hennesey, then Sam said:

'See to the horses, will you, Johnnie? It seems we have company.'

There was a dozen yards to cover to the house and the three moved across it in silence. Donovan had already got to his feet and with the added height the veranda gave him looked like a colossus as he stood, thumbs hooked in his belt and a half-smoked cigar in his mouth. Stone still lounged against the rail but the other four had come upright and Hennesey at least did not like the cold stare of the men.

'Like to talk to you privately, Stevens,' Donovan said.

'If it's business, and I can't think it'll be anything else, you'll have to include my sister.'

'I don't do business with women or girls.'

'Then you don't do any business with us, Mr Donovan.'

'All right, if you want it in public. I'm closing my land to you and your herds a week from today. That gives you a chance to get your stock and stuff away, unless you choose to stay here and starve.'

Stevens shook his head. 'We don't choose either way. That's free range and we've every right to drive over it, or for that matter graze our stock on it. If that's all you've come to say, Mr Donovan, then you've wasted your time. Now I'll be obliged if you take yourself and your crew off my land.'

'Not yet,' Donovan said ominously. 'Stone here has a little score to settle with your hired hand. It seems he took advantage of Stone's quiet nature.'

'You mean he licked an insulting bully,' Lucy flared at him. 'I reckon he could do it again too, at any time.'

'We'll see,' Donovan rasped. 'Harper, Savage, go and bring that young whelp over here. He somewhere's around the barns.'

As the pair slouched away, Hennesey said: 'What's your intentions, Mr Donovan? You've been invited to get off this land. Staying here is making trouble—' Hennesey hesitated. A brave enough man, he felt hog-tied under the hard-eyed stare of Morris and Dayley. He knew that if it came to gunplay, these two alone could outmatch him. There was Sam Stevens of course, but just how good he was with a gun, the marshal did not know. The other pair of gun-hawks would be back in a minute, too. Was it sensible to risk a showdown against such odds ? He had to admit to himself that it was not.

'You sounded as if you had something else you wanted to say,' Donovan sneered at him.

Hennesey met his gaze. 'I have, but I guess it will do another time. In plain words, Mr Donovan, I'm giving you no excuse for gunplay.'

Sam Stevens moved uncomfortably as his glance met the flaming anger in his sister's eyes. He saw now that Donovan wanted to provoke a fight. A fight that would be hopeless from the start with only his own and Hennesey's guns against those of the four professional killers. It would be that way, for Donovan himself would not bother to draw. Sam read the accusation of cowardice in Lucy's eyes, then his gaze shifted to Johnnie walking towards them between Harper and Savage. Stevens took a side glance at Stone, no longer lounging against the rail but now alert and with eyes filled with malevolence.

Johnnie came to a halt in front of Donovan. 'These fellers said you wanted to talk to me, mister.'

Donovan leaned forward in his saddle. What kind of a youngster was this Johnnie Callum who looked up at him without either fear or anger in his light blue eyes? Used to seeing either dislike or fear in the expressions of men who looked at him, Donovan felt irritated by Johnnie's almost friendly gaze.

'You know who I am and something about me?' Donovan boomed.

'I've heard about you, mister, and what I heard wasn't good, but the feller that told it me wasn't good either, so maybe he lied.'

'He didn't lie. Was your father's name Seth, mother, Louise?'

'That's right.'

'Then I'm the man that cleared them off my range. Now I'm going to clear you off, or at least, Stone is.' Donovan straightened again at the sudden change that came over Johnnie's face. He hated these always grinning sort of youngsters and now he had wiped the grin from this one's face. He motioned to Stone.

'Get your rope round this fellow and run him to hell out of this.'

The hands of both Hennesey and Stevens moved towards their guns but checked as Donovan's four gunslingers made similar moves.

Johnnie stood gazing at Donovan as if paralysed while Stone leisurely unhooked the lariat from his saddle. Then Johnnie's memory began to work. It slid swiftly through the years of misery he had spent with Manders and fastened on the night his parents' homestead had been stamped flat by a horde of yelling riders. He heard again the shouts of his father and the screams of his mother and suddenly their almost forgotten faces were vivid pictures to him. The paralysis left him and he saw only Donovan, big to almost giant size astride a horse that was equal to his weight. He noticed nothing of the casual coming forward of Stone, rope in hand, or of the tensed figures of Sam, Hennesey and Lucy in contrast to the relaxed but watchful stance of the gunhawks. Only Donovan was in his focus, and towards him he moved with a spring that had behind it all the power and swiftness of youthful limbs hardened and suppled by long hours of work. Stone was in the way of Johnnie's sudden leap and was shouldered aside like a straw. Donovan raised a surprised hand to ward off the attack, found it held in a grip that would not be shaken and cursed loudly as his frightened mount reared. He was almost out of the saddle before he managed to bring his fist down on the top of Johnnie's head with all the weight of his massive shoulders behind the blow. Johnnie grunted under the blow but there was no relaxing of his grip on Donovan's arm. The horse came down again and went into a sideways dance and again the big rancher came close to leaving the saddle. Then Donovan's bodyguard piled on to Johnnie, and the four pairs of hands bore him to the ground. He was in the process of being kicked to death when Hennesey and Stevens charged, their fists aiming blows right and left. The melee lasted only seconds and Donovan had sufficient to do in controlling his already scared mount to notice that in that time Lucy had darted indoors and reappeared with a Sharp's rifle in her hand. The first he or any of the men milling close to him knew of the business was the crack of a shot. The whine of the slug put an instant end to fist fighting and brought at the same time an instinctive turning towards the sound of the gun coupled with a reaching for weapons. Lucy's voice came as Donovan fought his mount to a standstill.

'That one was through your hat, Donovan. Keep yourself and your men quiet or the next will be through your head.'

There was no doubt in Donovan's mind that this usually quiet and well-behaved girl meant what she said and from the way she held the rifle ready to throw to her shoulder, of her capability to carry out the threat. He glanced at his four gunmen. They all seemed to be only too anxious to chance a quick draw and, of course, if they did so they would win out, but there was almost a certainty that he himself would be a dead man. He said, in a rasping voice:

'All right, Lucy. Your play for the time being. What do you want me to do?'

'Just tell Stone and those four other men to drop their guns and ride off.'

Donovan shrugged. 'As I said, it's your play now, but don't expect to be treated like a woman when we meet again. All right, boys, drop your guns. The girl has things running her way for the moment.'

Not until the five guns were on the ground did Lucy move her finger from the trigger of the rifle, then her stance relaxed and the muzzle of the gun lowered. Hennesey immediately drew his own gun and moved to Donovan.

'I'll take yours as well, Mr Donovan.'

Donovan handed him the weapon with a sneer. 'Never thought you'd be hiding behind a woman's skirts, Hennesey.'

'I've got to take that for the time being, but maybe next time we meet you won't be backed by four gunhands.'

Hennesey turned to one side and watched Stone and his four companions mount and ride away. Lucy had put down her rifle and, with Sam, was kneeling beside Johnnie. Hennesey saw the strain that was in the girl's face and wondered whether it came from Johnnie's condition or from the action she had just taken against the rancher. He wanted to go and see how the boy was, but thought it better to keep

51

an eye on Donovan in case he should get up to some trickery. Lucy, getting to her feet and running to the house and coming back with a tin basin of water and clean rags, told Hennesey that Johnnie was in a pretty bad way. He would have been walked to the house otherwise. His eyes went again to Donovan, now sitting his mount as if nothing unusual had happened and it came to him that an easy way out of this trouble would be to put a bullet through the man. It would be good sense even if it wasn't an honourable thing to do. Donovan, once released from here would be a man bent on vengeance. Sam and Lucy could not expect the week's grace he had originally given them. What they could expect was a night attack with guns and fire. The sort of thing Donovan had done to homesteaders and small ranchers in the past. For himself, Hennesey knew that he would have to walk the streets of the town with great care both by day and night.

Lucy got to her feet. 'Ed,' she called. 'You and Sam will have to carry him to a bed, we've done all we can here.'

Hennesey looked at Donovan. 'You can be on your way.'

'What about the guns?'

'Send someone over for them. I had thought of keeping you here for an hour and letting you take them with you, but it seems Johnnie needs a lot of help and I can't waste time watching you.'

Donovan started to turn his mount. 'You're adding up a big score, Hennesey. No one else has ever sent me away without my gun. In fact no one ever took it from me before.'

Hennesey shrugged. 'You can't do any more than kill me and that's a chance any marshal has to take.'

He moved to where Johnnie was lying and felt a little sick at what he saw. Although Lucy had cleaned the blood from the boy's face it still looked a terrible mess. Hennesey, who had seen something like it before, guessed that Johnnie had taken at least a dozen kicks about the head. He knelt down along with Stevens and together they carried Johnnie into the house and up to a bedroom. Stripped of his clothing, bruises showed on almost every part of his body. Hennesey, who was something of a doctor, checked that no bones were broken, but his efforts to rouse Johnnie to consciousness were unavailing.

'Have to leave him to sleep it off and just hope that his skull isn't cracked. Though we can't do anything if it is.'

'He's going to be pretty sick and sore for some time,' Sam said as they left the room. 'He took a tidy hammering in the few seconds those skunks were at him.' He looked at Lucy. 'Luce, that was smart and brave of you to go and grab that rifle. I reckon Johnnie would have been in a worse shape than he is now if it hadn't been for you.'

'Smart, perhaps, but not brave. My stomach was churning over when I lifted the rifle. But I saw that no one's eyes were on me and it seemed a good chance.'

Hennesey said, as they reached the living-room, 'I guess I don't have to warn you two to expect trouble after this. Maybe tonight. In fact I can only think of one thing that will stop it happening tonight.'

'That's more than I can do,' Sam said moodily. 'As I see it, Donovan has only got to ride back to town and collect some more men and guns and be back here in a couple of hours. Seems to me it's a matter of how long we can hold them off.'

'It is that way, Sam, except for one thing – vanity. What do you think those four gunhawks are going to feel like if they ride into town with empty holsters, Donovan himself for that matter. Can you see them standing for all the laughs when they try to borrow guns? You can take it from me they'd sooner be shot up.'

'I think you've got a point there, Ed,' Lucy said. 'It's more likely that Donovan will take his gunmen back home where they can get fresh weapons without attracting notice. That would mean they couldn't get back here before dawn.'

Sam shrugged. 'Well, allowing that you two are right. What have we got? Breathing space for one night. Maybe two. The thing is, Donovan is certain to come back and there'll be blood in his eyes when he does. Luce, I'm for getting out of here in the morning. We can take Johnnie with us in a rig.'

'Sam, you're trying to walk out because of me. Well, you can forget the idea. I'd stay even if I were here alone. No, the thing is to get Johnnie to some safe place. Then we can do our fighting without knowing we've a sick man on our hands. If Ed could have a rig sent from town in the morning we could ship Johnnie to some place of safety.'

'I wasn't figuring on going back to town,' Hennesey said. 'I had an idea of staying and fighting it out with you folks. I know that maybe doesn't sound like me. I mean bucking against Donovan.' His face went brick red. 'There have been times when I ought to have done it before but I reckon you knew how I was fixed when Donovan had a hold on the Silver Dollar and Luke Carter. One wrong move from me and I'd have been out of my job. Anyway, I've been thinking. I'm more or less certain that Donovan won't come back tonight and from what I've heard of him he won't stage an attack in the daytime, so I reckoned if I went back to town I might rustle up some help.'

'Well, I think it's a large sized might, Ed, but it's worth a try. In any case there's nothing to lose by it,' Sam said.

Hennesey moved towards the door. 'I'll get riding then, it'll be about dark when I reach town and I guess Donovan's boys'll be whooping it up as usual.'

CHAPTER FIVE

Hennesey turned his mount into the livery as soon as he reached town. Under the thin sliver of moon that was just rising the hitch rails appeared to be already packed with horses, and men were gathered in twos and threes, laughing, arguing and quarrelling noisily. The front of Carlen's store was crowded as was the lamp-lit space before Joe's eating bar, but it was on and around the veranda of the Silver Dollar under the spluttering kerosene flares that the pack of men was thickest. The marshal shouldered a good humoured way into the place and found it filled almost to bursting. Belle was moving in the throng of men, exchanging crude witticisms and stopping occasionally to chat briefly. Carter was at the top end of the room in conversation with Judge Bohun, and Hennesey made his way towards them.

'Hello, Ed. What'll you have to drink?' Bohun said between puffs at his cigar.

'Nothing at the moment, Judge. I want a serious talk with you and Luke. Has Donovan been back again, Luke?'

Carter shook his head. 'No, neither has Stone and the other four.'

Hennesey heaved a sigh of relief. 'Thank goodness for that. Judge, you're the man of law around here. I mean you can quote from the book. What can I do if one rancher threatens to clear another off the range?'

Bohun gave him a shifty look. 'Not much, Ed. The law don't take much account of threats. You could maybe have him before a court and the court might fine him fifty dollars or something like that.'

'Has Donovan come out in the open and threatened Sam and Lucy Stevens?' Carter asked.

'He has.' Hennesey sketched in briefly the happenings at the Stevens' ranch.

At his conclusion, Carter looked worried, Bohun apprehensive.

'We ought to give them some help,' Hennesey went on. 'I've been wondering if we couldn't raise a guard. Say half-a-dozen men.'

'A guard!' Bohun said. 'You mean fight back at Donovan? He can raise fifty men, more if he wants to.'

'I'm guessing that he won't send more than a dozen men for his first attack,' Hennesey argued. 'If they could be beaten off, Donovan won't find it so easy to raise a bunch for another attempt.'

'I get your point, Ed,' Luke said. 'You're figuring that out of all Donovan's men he can only really count on a dozen or so to engage in dirty work.'

'That's about it, Luke. Donovan has plenty of men who will follow if the going's not too tough. Fellers who would regard a little ranch warfare as part of the job, but I'm reckoning on them quitting as soon as they realize they're running against the law.'

'Well, I'll willingly stand the cost of half-a-dozen guards, Ed, but do you think you can raise that many?'

'For pay, yes. After all, they won't have to take a very big risk. I'd post them in the barns and places like that and armed with rifles they should be able to break up an attack. Particularly as Donovan's bunch won't be counting on much resistance. The thing is, I want the Judge to back the idea publicly. What do you say, Judge? If you made it known that you were backing me and would send for State help if necessary, don't you reckon that would hold Donovan back?'

Bohun puffed hard on his cigar and a trickle of perspiration ran down his fat face. He said, in an agitated voice:

'Ed, I think that the most dad-burned fool notion I ever heard of. Suppose your guards, if you can get any, do beat off Donovan's men and then I send for State help. How long do you think it'd be before any came? A month, maybe two, maybe never. Do you think Donovan will take a licking and then sit around and wait for another one? No, sir. If Donovan gets licked by men from this town, he's going to turn around and take this whole place to pieces. Nope, my business and yours, Ed, is to keep the peace in this town and we won't do it by promoting a range war. Ranchers have always fought over the ranges. I say, let them get on with it.'

Bohun's hand went towards his glass but Belle, who had come up unnoticed by the three men, snatched it from the table and threw the contents on the floor.

'Not another drop of liquor do you have in this house, Judge Bohun, not even if you want to pay for it, which you never do. I've been standing here for two or three minutes and I heard most of Ed and Luke said. Also I heard that darned speech of yours. Pah! Call yourself a judge. It's my opinion that back East you were some small-time lawyer who couldn't make a go of it, so like a lot more you come West and call yourself a judge and pick up whatever free living comes your way. If Ed's looking for guards to help out those Stevenses, he can count on me for one.'

Bohun's face went an angry red and the trickle of perspiration increased to a copious sweat. 'Belle, you've no call to talk in that insulting manner when a man is doing his best to give advice on a difficult matter.'

Hennesey, who saw that direct opposition from the judge might make a tough job even more difficult, said tactfully: 'The judge was only giving his opinion, Belle, even if he did give it a little forcefully. Maybe you'll let me buy him another drink.'

Her first flash of anger over, Belle sensed that Hennesey did not wish to antagonise the judge. She said, in a quieter voice:

'OK, Judge. Sorry I blew off. I'll get you another drink, but you other guys, no more scheming until I get back. In case you fellers have forgotten it, I've a sizeable stake in this town.'

She was back in a few seconds with Bohun's whiskey. 'Now,' she said to Hennesey. 'Set me up to date with the whole business.'

Hennesey told her and as he finished a sparkle appeared in Belle's green eyes. 'That Callum kid must be made of the right stuff. Feller, I'd sure have given plenty to have seen him busting into Donovan. That big hombre must have had the surprise of his life. I reckon, except for me sassin' him a few times, no one's ever said even boo to him. Luke, we ought to do something for young Callum, have him stay here for a start until he gets over that mauling.'

Carter gave a faint smile. 'Don't you think Donovan has enough stacked up against you already?' He turned to Hennesey. 'Ed, I've an idea where I might get men willing to stand guard on the Stevens' place. There are three families I know of who—'

Belle cut him off sharply with: 'Just a minute, Ed. Judge, after what you've just said are you behind this move of Luke's or against it?'

Bohun looked flustered. 'Well, like I said, Belle. I'm not in favour of starting a range war, but of course I wouldn't make any move against Hennesey or yourselves.' He got to his feet.

'Perhaps on the whole it would be better if I took my drink at the counter.'

Belle nodded. 'It might save some hard feelings, Judge.'

Bohun edged his way to the crowded bar and leaned against it in acute discomfort both from the press of noisy men around him and from the feelings working within him. Belle's jibe that he was not really a judge had struck deeper than she, or either of the two men, guessed. The fact was, he had been a judge until the ending of the civil war and, being a Southerner, had been hounded from his post by victorious Northerners. It had happened a good many years ago but the sore was still there, and Belle had probed deeply into it. Now, a hatred for her was working up within him. He finished the whiskey, and after some shouting of his order, got the sweating bartender to pour him another. The fact that he, a judge, had had to shout against rough range hands for his drink inflamed his anger, and he began to include Carter and Hennesey in his hatred. By the time he had emptied the whiskey glass again he was full of self pity and indignation. These three with their schemes would direct Donovan's anger against the whole town and, in particular, himself, as the foremost citizen. He saw himself being hounded out of the place by Donovan's riders, and grew almost maudlin in his self pity.

Then he saw a way that might prevent this thing from happening to him. He had guessed where Carter intended to get his guards, from the moment he had said: 'There are three families.' Yes, he was certain that he had guessed that rightly. Carter meant the Sanders, Regans and Thomases. All small rangers that Donovan, by one means or another had forced off the land, and all resettled near Leastown about sixty miles away. If a message could be got to Donovan warning him that a strong defence could be expected at the Stevens' place, then the rancher would be able to arrange his plans accordingly. How to get the message to Donovan was the difficulty. No use scribbling a note and giving it to one of the riders. By the time they were ready to leave town they would all be too drunk to be trusted as letter carriers. Besides, he did not want to openly involve himself in the matter.

Bohun thought for a long time, then heaved his bulk away from the bar and pushed a way out to the street. He went to his own neat, frame house and penned a short note that would tell Donovan what Hennesey intended to do. He left the note unsigned and sealed it into a stout envelope which he addressed in a large hand to Donovan. Bohun's next move was to the store and, as he expected, the MD rig was outside and partly loaded with stores. Bohun passed into the store and found Carlen busy at piling packages on to the counter. The storekeeper looked up.

'Hello, Judge. Something I can get for you?'

'Just some cigars, Carlen. I'm almost clean out of them. All this stuff for Donovan?' Bohun indicated the packages on the counter.

Carlen shot a stream of tobacco juice on to the floor. 'Sure is and a mighty fine time I'm having loading the stuff. Donovan's freight driver is supposed to give me a hand with the job but I guess he's got himself drunk. Here's your cigars.'

'Thanks.' Bohun picked up his own package, then lifted one of half-a-dozen boxes of cigars piled in front of him. 'I see Donovan smokes a mighty fine cigar. Genuine West Indian, eh?'

'Sure thing, Judge. About the best there is. Come as high as ten cents a piece. Well, I'd best get some of this stuff on to the rig or I'll be here all night.'

Bohun picked up the six boxes. 'I'll take these for you.' He laughed. 'Not much weight but it'll save you one trip.'

Between leaving the counter and getting to the rig, Bohun slipped the envelope from his pocket and put it underneath the topmost cigar box. He set the little pile of boxes carefully on the rig then with another jocular remark to Carlen waddled towards the Silver Dollar. It would be as well, he thought, if he could keep an eye on Hennesey, Carter and Belle in case there were any other moves afoot. In the saloon the noise was now almost deafening. Belle had seated herself at the tinny and out of tune piano and was pounding at a melody whilst half a dozen punchers grouped around her bellowed the song at full pitch. Hennesey was moving about the room, pausing now and again to watch the progress of one or the other of the poker games, but of Luke Carter there was no sign. Bohun got himself a drink then Hennesey saw him and moved towards him.

The marshal squeezed alongside the judge. 'Been out taking some fresh air?'

'Just along to the store for some cigars. I had a bit of a yarn with Carlen.'

'Should have thought he was too busy to spend time yarning.'

'Well, he was kind of. He was loading Donovan's stores. I didn't stay more than a minute or so.'

Bohun raised his glass to his lips and as he did so, the marshal's keen glance fastened on a small spot of ink on one of his fingers. The ink spot had not been there when Bohun had been seated with himself, Belle and Carter. Hennesey felt certain of that. He called for a mug of beer, got it after some delay and drank slowly. The judge, he noticed, was sweating a little. It could have been due to the heat of the place. On the other hand he had noticed that Bohun did perspire if he was nervous about anything. Deliberately not making any small talk, Hennesey let his mind dwell on the spot of ink and Bohun's visit to the store for cigars. The cigars were a fact all right. He could see the bulging shape of the package in Bohun's pocket.

Hennesey put his glass down. Something was wrong. The judge usually got his cigars at the bar, a few at a time and more often than not as a gift. Why had he gone to the store, where he would have to take a package of at least twenty-five, and pay cash for them?

Bohun was finding the silence difficult. 'Let's buy another drink and take it to one of the tables, Ed. My feet are killing me.'

'No thanks, Judge. I ought to be getting around the street for a while in case some of the boys are up to their usual tricks. Though up to now they've been orderly enough.'

Hennesey left the counter, pushed a way to the batwings and went straight towards the store. Carlen was busy serving three or four noisy punchers, and Hennesey, after a friendly caution to them, stepped outside to wait. The MD rig he saw was piled high with stores and wanted only the team and a driver. Carlen came out a few seconds later, shepherding the punchers in front of him. He mopped perspiration from his brow.

'Well, that's about it. Another month end nearly over. I wonder where the heck Donovan's driver got to? The pesky feller should have been here to help me load.'

'You have to do it all yourself, then?'

'Every darn package, barrel and sack. No, darn it, I forgot.' He laughed hoarsely. 'The judge carried out half-a-dozen boxes of cigars. Said it'd save me a trip. Bought some himself, too. I reckon he must have come into money.'

'Must have. I bet he put the cigars right where you wanted to plant a barrel of flour.'

'Nope, he acted real sensible. Put 'em right under the seat where they wouldn't get damaged.'

Hennesey stepped to the front of the rig and felt under

the seat. 'So he did. First time I've ever known him to do a heavy chore like that.'

Carlen laughed so much that he choked on his chew of tobacco and for a few seconds was bent head down, spitting and spluttering. Hennesey used the brief space of time to lift the cigar boxes into the light that came from the store lamps. The envelope dropped to the ground and with a quick move he scooped it up and stuffed it in his pocket. He was at Carlen's side and thumping him vigorously on the back without the storekeeper having noticed anything unusual about his movements. A few minutes later when Carlen was restored to his usual self, Hennesey walked towards his own office. In the light of the lamp he dragged the crumpled envelope from his pocket, read the address then hesitated before slitting the envelope open. Finally, he decided that his action was justified under the circumstances and he rapidly tore the envelope open and read the contents.

He spent the next few moments swearing under his breath. There could be no doubt who had written the note. Bohun's big, sprawling hand was easily recognisable. The thing was, what action should he take? Go directly to the judge and confront him with this piece of treachery. Or just keep quiet about it and look out for further moves from Bohun? He decided to keep the information to himself, not even tell it to Carter or Belle. For one thing, Belle would certainly have the matter in the open and that would be very little help. Still, it was going to be hell acting naturally when he met the judge. Knowing the man was weak and shifty was one thing but being aware that he would betray his friends was another.

Hennesey put the letter in a drawer of his desk, snuffed out the light and left the office. It was close to midnight and the least drunken of Donovan's riders were already leaving the town. The rest would have to be persuaded by his own efforts, seeing that neither Donovan or Stone were on hand. The idea caused him to grin a little. It did not matter to him if none of Donovan's riders got back to their work by morning, but he wanted the town clear as soon as possible so that he could make his way back to the Stevens' place. Luke Carter would be glad to see his saloon empty, too. Luke was taking the sixty-mile ride to Leastown the moment the Silver Dollar could close its doors.

CHAPTER SIX

In the late afternoon of the following day, Luke Carter led four other riders into the Stevens' place. No hard rider, Luke drooped in his saddle and was so stiff and sore he could barely heave himself out of the saddle. The four who had ridden in with him seemed scarcely affected by the sixty mile ride. They were Burt Sanders, tall and brown haired, Sean and Mike Regan, twin brothers, red of hair and with startlingly blue eyes, and Abe Thomas, fortyish and sun dried to the toughness of good leather. Thomas had raised cattle in a small way until Donovan had forced him off the ranges, whilst the two Regans and Sanders were sons of homesteading families that had been ruthlessly driven from their lands by MD riders. All four had a burning desire to pull Donovan's empire down.

Sam and Lucy Stevens came out on to the veranda as the thud of hoofs reached them. There were greetings, expressions of surprise at the way the Regan brothers and Sanders had grown from youths into tough young men in the seven or eight years since the parties had last met and on the part of the new arrivals a good deal of remarking on the fact that Lucy had grown from a pigtailed child into a young woman of considerable attraction. After that there was the business of seeing to the weary horses, then a deal of sluicing

65

away the riders' own dust and grime. A substantial meal followed with hardly a word spoken about the business in hand. Then with tobacco smoke curling up to the rafters of the big living-room Sam said:

'Lucy and I want to thank you fellows for coming. We hadn't figured on asking help to fight Donovan, that was Luke's idea.'

'Think nothing of it,' Thomas cut in. 'We should have banded together years back. If we'd done that us fellers might have still been on this part of the land. Luke's been telling us about Donovan's latest moves and the only thing we want to do is put an end to them, fast.'

'Yes, what's the plan?' Sanders asked.

Sam gave a thin smile. 'I'm afraid there isn't much of a plan. Hennesey was out here this morning and the best we could think of was to post a guard, say two men, about a quarter of a mile from the house. You fellows will have noticed when you rode in here that the going is pretty rough. In the dark, and Donovan usually has his dirty work done then, there's only a narrow strip, say about a mile wide, that is reasonable for riders. Ed and I reckoned two men could watch that strip and if they see anything, sound off a shot. In the house here, four guns could hold off an army.'

'That's so,' Thomas said. 'Your Paw was pretty wise when he built this place in stone and only had small windows. Of course there were Indians about then.'

'I'm not much of a hand with a gun,' Carter put in, 'but I guess I can make a row with one.'

'We weren't reckoning on your gun, Luke,' Sam said. 'Lucy was in the four. Hennesey wants you to get back to your own place. Tonight, if you can manage it.'

'Tonight! Heck, I'm that sore and stiff I can hardly sit a chair, never mind a saddle.'

'We'll fix you up with a buggy and a cushion on the seat,'

Lucy smiled.

'Yes, that's right,' Sam agreed. 'The thing is, Luke, Hennesey wants someone in town he can trust. He didn't say exactly why, but I gathered that he is more than suspicious of something the judge has been up to.'

Carter got to his feet. 'In that case I'd best be going. I don't want to be on the trail after sundown. By the way, Luke, how's young Callum coming along?'

'He was awake for about half an hour at noon,' Lucy said. 'He seemed a little delirious but I think he's going to be all right. Perhaps a week or two in bed will set him right. I hope so, he took a terrible beating.'

'Callum,' Thomas said. 'That was the name of those sodbusters Donovan stamped out. I wonder what became of them.'

'Johnnie believes they're dead,' Lucy said quietly. 'I suppose it's best not to disturb the belief although from the time he learned from Donovan that he was the man who had cleared his parents from the land, Johnnie seemed set on doing murder. I only hope he doesn't hold to the idea when he gets on his feet again.'

'Well, they may be dead for all we know,' Thomas said. 'The only thing I know is there was no sign of life on the place when I rode over in the dawn. I didn't dare go before that although I could see the blaze from their place and knew darned well what was happening.'

'Much the same thing that happened to my Paw and Maw,' Burt Sanders growled angrily. 'I wasn't much more than a kid at the time but I remember the shooting and burning all right.'

'There's two of us here with the same sort of remembrances,' Sean Regan said with quiet emphasis, 'and I guess Mike and I would sure like to shake hands with this Johnnie Callum. He must have real guts to fly at a man the size of Donovan and him with four killers to back him up.'

'I'm with you there, all the way,' Mike said angrily. 'Sure, I wish my own hands were big enough to tear the murdering skunk apart.'

Carter moved stiffly towards the door. 'Show me this buggy, Sam, and the best of luck to all of you.'

With Carter on his way to town and the Regan brothers posted in the best position for guarding the house there was nothing to do but to settle down to the grim business of waiting and in the meantime carrying on with as much of the routine work of looking after the ranch as was possible. The waiting lasted for three nights with Sanders and Thomas alternating with the Regans as outside guards. It was a wearing business and perhaps doubly so for Lucy who did not have a man's natural thirst for fighting. She found some relief in the fact that on the second day of waiting, Johnnie, after waking normally in the morning, insisted on getting out of bed before noon. He was wobbly on his legs but to the surprise of herself and Sam, rapidly gained a little strength. It seemed to her natural that he should at first be without his cheerful smile, but on the following day there was little doubt in her mind that Johnnie was brooding. Sam and the other men noticed it too and put it down to Johnnie's desire for vengeance either on the men who had so brutally mauled him or on Donovan for his treatment of Seth and Louise Callum. They were right only in part. Johnnie wanted vengeance on Donovan for the parents he hardly remembered and only the big rancher's death would suffice. Yet he fought against the desire to kill Donovan. Fought it with all his will, because after the way he had dealt with, first, Josh Manders and then Stone, he regarded himself as a natural killer, something near a maniac. He had seen both men through a red haze when fighting them and that fact coupled with the knowledge that he had little detailed memory of either struggle was convincing enough to him. A few words spoken by an older and wiser man would have cleared the whole thing from his mind, but Johnnie kept his ideas to himself and none of the others tried to probe into them.

He was in bed but wide awake on the fourth night of the watch when the single shot sounded. He moved quickly and was, of those resting, first to get down to the living-room. Stevens, who was checking weapons that were on the table under a shaded light, said:

'Pick which guns you like, Johnnie.'

Johnnie hesitated a moment. 'I never used a gun before, Sam. I don't know if I can shoot.'

'Never used a gun!' There was real surprise in Sam's voice.

'No. Manders had an old shot-gun but he wouldn't let me go near it.'

Lucy and Thomas entered the room in time to hear the discussion. Sam was about to say something else when a second shot split the quiet of the night and there followed a rattle of six-gun shots.

'Battle's started,' Sam said quickly. 'Thomas, will you take that landing window? It's the only one upstairs that looks on the back of the house. Sanders and I will take the front bedrooms. Lucy, keep to the living-room and see that you're well behind the shutters. Don't poke a gun too far through the loop-holes. It might give your position away.'

He and the other two men raced for the stairs just as a tattoo of slugs beat into the stout front door. Lucy picked up a Springfield. Then she regarded Johnnie calmly.

'You'll have to learn to shoot some time, you know.'

Johnnie nodded. 'I wish I'd learned before, but I didn't get a chance.'

'Well, we'll start now.' She levered the shells out of a second Springfield and handed it to him. 'Now throw it up to your shoulder, like this.' She demonstrated the movement.

Johnnie made a few awkward movements with the gun then started visibly as a patter of shots rattled against the shutter.

'I ought to be outside doing something to chase those guys off,' he said.

'Johnnie, these men would kill you as easy as killing a running hen. You wouldn't get a chance to use those big fists of yours. Now try again. It'll soon come to you. Then I'll show you about the sights and the loading.'

Johnnie tried desperately hard and five minutes later found himself at a loop-hole with a loaded gun to his shoulder. The last instruction he got from Lucy was to squeeze the trigger if he saw anything moving. He stood for three whole minutes with the rifle gripped so hard that his fingers began to ache. His eyes tried to differentiate between the various shadows between the house and the barns while part of his mind tried to digest and act upon all the advice that Lucy had just given him. The other part was occupied by the fact that from the men upstairs there was almost continual firing and from Lucy there was a shot every few seconds. Was there no attack on the rear of the house or was he so unused to this business that he could not see men who crept along in the dark? Then his face reddened. Of course there was no attack on this side of the house. Lucy had placed him here because he was useless at gun fighting. With his hands, perhaps, and when he lost his temper and had that red mist in front of his eyes but with a gun of any kind, no. The rifle relaxed in his grip and he was on the point of putting it down and turning away from the shutter when there was a bang that he heard above the others and the scream of a slug accompanied by a rending noise above his head. He was aware, without knowing it properly, that his shutter was being fired at, and the rifle firmed again in his big hands. His mind cleared and Lucy's instruction came to him calmly and lucidly. 'Hold the gun well into your shoulder. Don't grip too hard. Get the fore sight in the middle of the back sight and your target on top of the fore sight. Then squeeze the trigger.'

And there was a target, a man who had moved swiftly from the shadow of the bunkhouse to the slighter shadow cast by the windmill pump. A man who carried something bulky under one arm and seemed bent on reaching the horse barn. Two more slugs ripped through the shutter and the fusillade from upstairs reached to a greater capacity. Then the man with the bundle moved. He went at a run towards the horse barn and for a moment he seemed to stand on Johnnie's gun sights. Only for a moment but it seemed minutes to Johnnie before he could steady himself into slowly squeezing the trigger. He felt the Springfield kick against his shoulder, then from outside came an explosion that made the stout walls of the house shudder whilst the darkness in front of Johnnie was split with a blinding, white light. There followed a blast of air that sent Johnnie reeling. The single light on the table snuffed out and where the shutter had been, a square of starlit sky showed. Dazed though he was, he reacted to Lucy's cry of alarm and jumped to her side.

'What was that, Johnnie?'

Her hand gripping on his arm brought a feeling that was new to him. A sense that he was needed. He felt the desire to protect this slender girl who clung to his arm and knew an exultation in his own size and strength.

'I don't know, Lucy. I saw a man running with something in his arms and fired, just like you told me.'

There was a sound of feet running down the stairs and Sam rushed into the darkened room. 'That blast was dynamite,' he shouted. 'The front door's off its hinges.'

He turned and ran back into the hall, Johnnie and Lucy

following close on his heels. The heavy door was flat on the floor and the hall a swirl of dust. There was no shooting now and the silence seemed ominous after the racketing of the guns. Sam and Johnnie lifted one end of the door and had it half raised when a single shot broke the silence and Sam, with a cry of pain, dropped his side of the door and fell backwards. Johnnie, overbalanced by the sudden shift of weight, found himself falling sideways. He dropped his hold on the door and fell on top of it as a six-gun hammered shots through the opening. Sprawled as he was on the floor he got a clear, skyline silhouette of the man using the gun. He felt rage surge within him, rage at the fact that Lucy was somewhere behind him and in peril from the slugs that sang low over his own head. He came bounding up from his sprawled position with the red mist of fury swimming in front of his eyes. The gunman was fifteen or twenty yards from the doorway when Johnnie came leaping out and directed his last two shots at the figure that was flying towards him. Johnnie felt the wind of one slug fan his cheek and for some reason saw clearly again. The rage was still with him when he closed with the man, but it was clear-headed anger, one that enabled him to swerve and evade the clubbed sixgun that the other swung at his head. He took the gunman at waist level and his long arms wrapping round the man, lifted him from his feet and dashed him to the ground. Johnnie followed up by diving on top of the gunslinger, received a knee jab in the stomach as his left hand reached the other's throat, then he was astride the man and his bunched right fist was punching the other into insensibility.

In a minute or two he got to his feet, satisfied that the other was unconscious. He heard guns begin again their erratic banging and saw the red flashes coming from the house. Then came the pounding of hoofs and he saw the silhouettes of four riders gallop past the shattered door and fill the space with their lead. Instinct, more than any knowledge of gunfighting, told him that the riders would circle the house and repeat the manoeuvre. Sharply aware of the danger of being shot by one of the defenders, Johnnie swung away from the direct line of the doorway and made a rush towards the house. He came to a crouch at the side of the veranda just as someone in the upper storey took two quick rifle shots at him. He had barely recovered from his forward rush when the hoofs sounded again and almost on the top of the sound he caught sight of the shadowy figure of the first of the riders. He let horse and man come almost abreast of him then left the ground in a long leap. He grabbed at the bridle and as the horse plunged and swerved, lifted his feet clear of the ground. He heard the oaths of the rider then a gun banged close to his head. The horse he was clinging to reared as far as his weight on its bridle permitted, then another horse thudding into it sent it staggering and pawing for a footing. For the next few seconds it seemed to Johnnie as he clung fiercely to the bridle, that the world was full of stamping horses, swearing men and guns that were being fired close to his head. Then the bridle broke and he hit the ground with a bump, saw hoofs that were apparently going to stamp him flat and rolled quickly to one side. A moment later he was on his feet and throwing wild punches at the head of a man who hit him so often with bunched up fists that it seemed to Johnnie that his adversary possessed more than one pair of arms. He made several attempts to close with the man and wrap him with his arms but each time a savage punch slammed him backwards. Guns were still banging but the racket of them went unheeded by the milling pair as they stamped about. Johnnie went down to a blow on the side of the head that caught him as he was boring in for about the twentieth time. He came bouncing to his feet again and rushed at his man who was standing with a slight forward droop, arms pendant as if he was too weary to raise them. Johnnie heard, as he closed in, the man's gusty, laboured intake of breath and the sound filled him with glee. He had this man beaten to a standstill and had done it without losing his own head. He chopped down the other's feeble guard and for the first time in his life aimed a timed and directed punch. It took his adversary just under the ear and he dropped like a poleaxed steer.

Johnnie stood for a moment gazing down on the man he had felled. He was so filled with satisfaction at having punched this man to the ground that he failed to notice either that the dawn was steadily spreading across the sky or that there was now no sound of guns. It was Sam's shouts that jerked him to the present and turned his head towards the veranda. There he saw Sam and Lucy standing with Burt Sanders and Abe Thomas. All four had rifles in their hands but their grips were relaxed as if they no longer needed the weapons. Johnnie saw the reason why as he moved towards them and he sickened a little at the sight of four obviously dead men sprawled a few paces from a dead horse. Of the four on the veranda, only Lucy was not entirely jubilant at their victory. She had little to say but watched Johnnie critically as the others slapped him on the back and proclaimed him as a great fighter. It took Johnnie a few minutes to understand that it was his pulling to a standstill of the horse and rider that had really turned the battle in their favour. In his own excitement he had not seen the confusion it had caused among the other riders or been aware that Sam and Lucy in the doorway had been provided by his action with easy targets. The Regan brothers coming up to the veranda made it necessary for a fresh telling of Johnnie's efforts and in the middle of that the rider who had been knocked out got uncertainly to his feet. He saw the group on the veranda, hesitated for a moment, then walked towards them.

Sam eyed him grimly. 'Jeff Talbot, I didn't think to see you in on a business like this. I've a notion to drop you where you stand.'

Talbot eyed the ground in front of him. 'Didn't want to come, Sam, but you know how it is. Donovan gives orders and we're kinda scared to refuse to carry them out.'

'Even if it means someone's death. Maybe your own as well,' Sam said sourly. 'Well, there's a message you can take to Donovan and anyone else that fancies clearing us off the range. You won't have to say anything, just take these four dead men back to MD and everyone will understand what I mean.'

'There's two more a little ways out,' Mike Regan cut in. 'Me and Sean got ourselves one each.'

'Six dead!' Sam exclaimed. 'That makes the price of land grabbing pretty high. Talbot, how many were in your raiding party?'

'Ten. Harper was supposed to be leading us.'

Sean's eyes ranged over the four corpses in front of the house. 'Harper ain't among that lot. I'd know those fancy stitched boots of his a mile off. He ain't one of those we got either. Looks like Harper will be able to tell the news to Donovan himself.'

'Just the same, we'll load these bodies into a rig and Talbot can drive them back to MD. Digging graves might cool down any others who want to carry out Donovan's orders.'

'I'll go harness a rig up,' Johnnie said.

'You'll do no such thing,' Lucy told him sharply. 'For a man who's only just gotten over one mauling, you've done enough for the time being. You get inside the house and I'll bathe as many of those bruises on your face as I can count.'

Johnnie grinned, then his face set into hard lines. He

faced about to Talbot. 'I've got a message for Donovan as well. Tell him that Johnnie Callum had almost forgotten about his parents until the other day. Then say that I'm taking up their old patch of land as soon as I can locate it.'

CHAPTER SEVEN

Harper reached the MD spread just after dawn. There were three other riders with him but none of them had anything to say to him. They were ordinary range hands with no pretensions to being gunmen and had little liking for the night's business they had been engaged on. They had gone to the Stevens' place because Donovan had given the order and they considered range warfare as part of their ordinary job, but now they were filled with disgust both for themselves and for Harper who had been their leader in what was supposed to be the comparatively simple job of cleaning up a small timer. Shooting up the place so that the occupants of it would turn and flee in terror they thought of as comparatively harmless, although of course there was the chance that someone would get killed in the process, but using dynamite did not amount to fair play. The three had been genuinely shocked when Harper had produced the dynamite from a sack he carried and told them of his intention to blow, first, the horse barn and then the house, and had refused to have anything to do with the idea. Harper had threatened and cajoled, then finally turned the job over to Morris, with Dayley and Savage to give him covering fire. Morris had died terribly in the attempt and the only result had been shattered windows and doors to the house. Still, it looked as if it had made it easier to throw enough lead into the house to scare the defenders into running and the three had taken their part in circling the place and pumping shots into it, then out of it had come the madman who had pulled one horse to a stop and thrown the rest into a confusion. A confusion that had left three dead men. Harper had been elsewhere when the dynamite exploded prematurely and was similarly out of the way when the three riders had been shot down. It looked to the men who climbed from their saddles at the same time that Harper did, suspiciously like cowardice.

Harper himself knew it was cowardice and wondered how he could explain the failure of the enterprise to Donovan without disclosing the fact. It was a peculiarity of Harper's make-up that although he could stand with an unwinking stare within ten paces of any man who wanted to draw against him, he could not face up to the wild shooting that went on in a general battle between men. Conscious of the hostility of his companions, Harper left them and walked across to Donovan's huge, stone and log-built house. Donovan stepped out on to the porch at his knock on the door.

'Well?' There was neither friendliness nor compromise in the rancher's booming tones.

'We didn't do too good, Boss.'

'How'd you mean? You didn't do too good.'

'There was more men than we expected. I guess a dozen. There was five or six of our men killed and—'

'Five or six ! Hell's bells. Don't you know what went on? How many men rode back with you?'

'Three, Boss, but it was that dark—' Harper realized he had made a trap for himself.

Donovan took a step forward until he was almost against Harper. 'Four of you came back, eh? and ten of you went and you don't know for certain whether they're alive or dead? Harper, that makes you a lily-gutted coward, the sort I don't want around here. Now get the hell off my ranch.'

Harper's face went livid and immediately he made a lightning grab for his gun. 'No man calls me coward—' he began, when Donovan's massive fist smashing into his mouth ended both the quick draw and the speech at the same time as it sent him grovelling in the dust.

Donovan, moving quickly in spite of his bulk, drove a boot into Harper's ribs then stooped and snatched the six-gun from his holster. He stepped back a pace and cocked the gun.

'Now get going before I drill a hole between your ugly eyes.'

Harper picked himself up painfully and hobbled away and Donovan stalked towards the bunkhouse. He found the three riders who had come back with Harper and wrung from them a halting story of the night's events as far as it was known to them. In a black rage at the seemingly easy defeat of his men, he went back to the house and flung himself heavily into a chair on the veranda. For a while he chewed on an unlit cigar then after a time the anger faded from his face. Of course, he had acted too quickly, that was all. Stevens, after the way he had threatened the man, had got himself help from somewhere to guard his place. He had only to wait, perhaps a week, perhaps two, and the guards would get tired of sitting around and go back to where they came from. An alternative was to find out who they were and arrange raids on their places. A night firing or something like that would send them scuttling fast enough. He tossed away the chewed cigar, took another from his pocket and lit it. Yes, a little patience was all that was needed and he would superintend the next raid on the Stevens' place himself. He smoked for a while then jerked his head round at the sound of wheels rumbling nearby. His first impulse was to curse at the driver of the rig for bringing it so close to the house, then he saw Hennesey riding alongside the rig and he got to his feet. Hennesey, a rare enough visitor, could only spell trouble of some kind.

The rig stopped a few yards away and both the driver and Hennesey got down to the ground. They covered the remaining space slowly, like men with something heavily on their minds. Hennesey spoke first.

'Mr Donovan, there's six of your riders in that rig. All of them dead from gun shots, except one. He was killed in an explosion and there isn't very much left of him. Talbot here gave me the story and said they were acting on your orders. I'm asking you if such is the case.'

'You're asking me! Well I must say you've got more sand in you than I ever reckoned on. What makes you think you'll get an answer from me, Mr Marshal?'

'I didn't think I would get an answer. Just hoped, that's all. If I can't get an answer I'll have to leave it to higher authority. I'll make myself plain, Mr Donovan. If you were any other man I'd take you in and charge you with promoting a range war and attempted murder.'

'But being me, you're afraid.'

'I guess you could put it that way. I know darned well I can't arrest you and if I could I wouldn't be able to hold you.'

'You're damned right you couldn't. What the hell made you come here?'

'To give you a chance to quit on this range war before I send for State help.'

'State help! So that's your game. I suppose you reckon on that so-called judge backing your plea. Well, you can get to hell from here and tell Bohun that I can block any of his attempts to bring troopers this way. As for you, Talbot, I'll find ways of teaching you that it doesn't pay to go snivelling to the marshal.'

'You've got things the wrong way round,' Hennesey said. 'Bohun isn't backing my idea for State help and Talbot didn't come snivelling to me. I saw him coming through town with that rig and forced the story from him.'

Donovan grinned. 'So you're on your own, eh? Talbot, you take that rig away and have some men help you with the burying. I'll see you later. Hennesey, I advise you to get to blazes out of this and think things over.'

As Hennesey mounted and rode away, Donovan dropped back into his chair. For almost an hour he sat thinking. Hennesey, since Belle had regained control of the saloon, was a different man, a man to be reckoned with. He would undoubtedly ask for State help and Donovan was not at all sure that he could block the application in spite of the fact that he was paying certain officials heavily not to pry too closely into his land grabbing dealings. The thing to do was get rid of Hennesey before he sent his message asking for help. The odds were that that message would go by the stage, in three days from now. Could he find a way of getting rid of Hennesey before that happened? For a moment, Donovan regretted his hasty dismissal of Harper. He would have been just the man to force a quarrel on the marshal then beat him to a quick draw. Either one of the other three gunslingers would have been equal to the task, of course, but as he had not seen them he presumed they formed part of the rig's grisly load. A pity he himself had lost control of the Silver Dollar. If he had hung on to that it would have been easy to have Hennesey fired. The notion set his mind on a fresh track. Why should whoever owned the saloon have the hiring and firing of the town's marshal? Only because the remaining property owners in the town were either too poor or too disinterested to pay the marshal's wages. Suppose he, himself owned most of the property, that would give him a right to a say in the marshal's appointment or his dismissal. Donovan got to his feet and strode towards the horse corral. There he saw Talbot and called the man to him.

'Get that big sorrel saddled for me. I'm going into town.'

Talbot said: 'Yes, Boss,' then hesitated.

'Well, what are you waiting for?' Donovan snarled.

'I had a sort of message for you, Boss. I forgot 'til now. Sam Stevens said that you or anyone else that fancied clearin' him off the range would understand what those six dead men meant. Then a youngster named Johnnie Callum said to tell you that he'd almost forgotten about his parents until the other day, and he's goin' to take up the patch of land they held as soon as he can locate it. I didn't understand what he meant but that's about what he said.'

Donovan grunted. 'I understand all right, the conceited young pup. Now get that horse saddled.'

Donovan reached town an hour before noon and pulled up outside Judge Bohun's house. He looped his reins over the picket fence and thudded his fist on the door. Bohun, freshly shaved but without his collar, opened the door. He gave Donovan a surprised look in which there was a hint of fear. He stood aside to let the rancher enter.

'You got my message, then ?' he said as he led the way into the parlour. 'I thought you'd know my handwriting.'

'Message! What message?'

Bohun paled, realizing that something had gone wrong. His first thought on seeing Donovan was that he had had the message, had recognised in spite of the lack of signature that it had come from him and that Donovan was here to thank him for it. He said nervously:

'I guess it doesn't matter seeing as you didn't get it.'

'What the blazes are you talking about?' Donovan barked, 'Come on, out with it.'

The judge swallowed hard then reeled off a detailed account of how he had attempted to send a warning message to Donovan between the boxes of cigars. 'I didn't sign the note, fortunately,' he concluded.

'Fortunately, maybe,' Donovan said drily. 'Whoever got

the note will most likely recognise your handwriting but won't be able to prove it yours. The thing is, will the fellow need proof or will he go after you with a gun? Supposing the note got into the hands of Stevens? Do you think he would need more proof than he got from his own eyesight? Anyway, you did your best and had the right idea in your head. A range war is no part of the town's business. I guess if you had the running of the town, you'd fire that Hennesey feller.'

Bohun nodded. 'I reckon I would. It doesn't make sense to me to plague the biggest outfit in the district when the town's dependent on it for its trade.'

'Then run it for me,' Donovan urged. 'Listen, I need a man like you, one who knows the law and can use it for me. Tell me. How would I stand, supposing I bought all the property I could lay my hands on. Would that give me a say in appointing a marshal?'

Bohun took time to consider the question. 'In the absence of any other authority, the owners of property have a right to appoint a marshal. That's the way it's been here only that Carter owns the biggest block of property, the Silver Dollar, and no one else has bothered. There have been cases where a town has had two marshals. Not for long, of course.'

'Just as long as it took one to shoot the other,' Donovan said. 'Well, maybe it'll turn out that way in this town. I want you to act as my agent. Buy every piece of property you can. Offer a good price and let me know if there are any non-sellers.'

Bohun drew in his breath sharply. 'You mean buy up the town? Hell, that'll cost you plenty. No matter how quietly I go to work it's bound to come out that you're buying then the prices will jump a mile high.'

'Pay them, whatever they are, and I want it all done in the next two days. Make it clear to everyone that they can stay on at a nominal rent, promise anything but get me the town.'

A nervous sweat broke out on Bohun's forehead. He asked

a few questions concerning the supply of cash, managed to think of a suitable percentage for himself then, as Donovan was impatient to be gone, showed the rancher to the door. Closing the door after Donovan, the judge hastened inside again to put on his collar and shoestring tie. A few minutes later he was on his way to the Silver Dollar feeling that nothing but a large sized glass of real whiskey would still the excitement he was feeling. He had redeye in the house but felt it was hardly the proper drink for one who in a few days' time would be the most influential citizen in Carterville, except perhaps for Luke Carter.

Belle Clancy, Carter and Hennesey were in conversation with the youth that Bohun remembered had hired to Stevens when Bohun rolled his bulk up to the bar. He gave them an all-embracing nod as he ordered his whiskey, but wanting to savour both the drink and his excitement, made no attempt to join the group. Carter, however, hailed him with:

'A moment, Judge. There's something you might be able to set us right about.'

Bohun frowned but took his whiskey and joined the group. 'Something about law?' he asked.

'Not quite,' Carter answered. 'This is Johnnie Callum, Judge. Does the name mean anything to you?'

'Callum, Callum. Let me see now. Yes, I've got it. There was a family of that name who homesteaded south-east of here. Be about seven or eight years back, I guess. You looking for them, young feller, relations of yours, eh?'

Hennesey cut in before Johnnie could frame an answer. 'Just exactly where was the place, Judge?'

Bohun took a gulp of whiskey. 'Easy enough to find, Marshal. You know that place the boys call Chimney Rock? The river sort of bends sharply round it and there's a way to climb down to the water. Well, it was just about there. Shouldn't be surprised if there's signs of the soddy there yet.

Although I guess Donovan's—' Bohun stopped suddenly, flushed and then went on. 'What the heck does anyone want to know that for, anyway?'

'I wanted to know,' Johnnie said woodenly, 'because that soddy belonged to my parents and I'm going to take the place for my own.'

'Now look here, son,' Bohun said quickly. 'You don't want to try any foolishness like that. The land that way belongs to Donovan. I guess you've heard of him, he's the biggest rancher for a hundred miles around here and he doesn't stand for any nonsense. Hennesey, you ought to tell this young feller to get the crazy notion out of his head before he gets himself killed.'

'Before Donovan's men kill him, you mean? Yes, I've told him about that. Now I'm asking you what title, if any, Donovan has to that land. Seems to me from my maps that it's free range.'

'Free to those who have enough guns to hold it,' Belle snapped. 'Hennesey, you know darned well that Donovan hangs on to what he's stolen because he can pay for plenty of gunslingers. The judge knows it as well, only he's scared to say so. If Johnnie, here, is going to buck against Donovan then I'm all for him and I wish others would follow his lead.'

'Belle, talk sense,' Hennesey pleaded. 'I'm doing my best to keep Donovan in line but he's big and has plenty of guns. If Johnnie squats on that land, it will end with him being killed.'

Johnnie glanced from one to the other. 'I'm thanking you folks for helping me find out what I wanted to know and I'll be getting back to Sam Stevens. He needs plenty of help yet, but just as soon as he can spare me, I'll be settling on my land.'

'For heaven's sake, Johnnie, drop the idea,' Carter said. 'At least until someone pulls Donovan down to his proper size.'

'Someone,' Belle snapped. 'Always someone. Somebody big enough. Well, I think Johnnie's big enough from what Ed's told us. All he needs is some help and by glory I'm going to give him plenty.' She turned her green eyes on Johnnie. 'Why aren't you totin' a gun, young feller?'

'Haven't got one, ma'am. Wouldn't know how to use it if I had one.'

'Cut out the ma'am and call me Belle, everyone else does. Now come down to the store with me and we'll fix about a gun.'

Johnnie shook his head. 'I haven't got as much money as that, Belle.'

'Shucks, you'll have plenty some day. Pay me for it then.'

She hustled Johnnie out of the saloon and left the others talking. Bohun chatted for a while and picked up a few details of what had taken place at the Stevens' ranch house. Details that were sparse because they had come to the marshal from Johnnie and Talbot, but nevertheless showing that the boy was something of a fighter. In the short period of listening, the judge thought he detected some reluctance on the part of the marshal to speak freely and guessing that it was he who had come into possession of the note intended for Donovan, left the place. He met with Belle and Johnnie leaving the store and saw that the youngster had a .45 Colt in a holster tucked under his arm. He gave a nod to the pair and passed into the store himself. Carlen, he knew, had often talked about going East into retirement if he could get a good price for his store and with that knowledge in his head it took him less than a quarter of an hour to effect a purchase. Moss, who owned the small livery, was a different proposition. He loved his business and was hardly tempted by a substantial offer. Finally, Bohun concluded a bargain that gave the ownership of the place to Donovan but left Moss the full running of the place. An hour later, gossip in the town was only on one subject. Bohun was buying up property and paying good prices. By nightfall, with the exception of a few shacks whose owners would not sell, the Silver Dollar was an island in a town owned by Donovan. Bohun, who had at first concealed the fact that he was buying for Donovan had, early on in the business, given up the idea. He found it hopeless to sustain the deception in the faces of so many who knew that he was continually hard up for money. The one thing he did manage to keep to himself was Donovan's reason for buying.

Carter, Belle and Hennesey discussed the matter until midnight but reached no other conclusion except that whatever motive Donovan had, it would be a bad one. Johnnie drove into the Stevens' place about sundown and in the middle of unloading stores gave Sam and Lucy snippets of news. Johnnie gave his news in the order of its importance to himself. First, he knew where his parents soddy had been, second, he now had a Colt .45 which he would learn to use, and a very poor third was the item that Bohun was buying property for Donovan. All his listeners raised eyebrows at that piece of information but made no more of it than those in the Silver Dollar had done. It was something bad but how bad they could not figure out.

The last of the daylight over the Stevens' outfit found Johnnie practising hard with his new weapon and soaking up advice from the Regan brothers.

Lucy watched with a troubled frown on her brow. Somehow, Johnnie's intention to take over the place his parents had been evicted from worried her more than did the plight she and Sam were in. At the moment the only bright spot she could see on her horizon was the fact that Johnnie had said he would not quit them as long as Donovan remained a menace. It seemed to Lucy, somehow better that they should all go down together, if that was to be the way of things, rather than Johnnie should be on his own when the rancher struck.

CHAPTER EIGHT

Saturday was stage day for Carterville with the coach due about two in the afternoon. Hennesey wakened to the day with an uncertain mind. Literally nothing had happened in the town since Donovan had bought the place over. Nothing had happened on the Stevens' place either. Was he, therefore, justified in sending a letter by the stage to appeal for State help? Or rather, would officialdom take any notice of such an appeal? After all, it would be based on one defeated raid on the Stevens' plus a lot of complaints about what had happened in past years – the years when land-grabbing and burnings-out hardly meant news. Hennesey had practically decided to abandon the idea when he came out into the bright, morning sunshine. A rig was trundling down the street, a fact that surprised him a little, it being too early for the store to be open. Then he saw that the two men on the sprung seat were Donovan's men and his surprise increased. The rig must have left the MD well before dawn to have reached town by now. He watched the vehicle draw up outside the judge's house and the men climb down. One of them reached out a spade and began to dig a hole in Bohun's front patch of grass and weeds. A few minutes later they dragged a yard square noticeboard from the rig and planted the post of it in the hole. With the hole filled in again, the rig rolled towards the far end of the street. Hennesey crossed to the front of the judge's house and his eyebrows lifted when he read the painted notice.

DONOVAN CITY

Temporary Office of the Marshal.
Judge Bohun, Temporary Marshal.

Underneath a paper was pinned announcing that election of a marshal would take place at noon in front of the judge's house and that all were entitled to vote. Donovan's signature was scrawled on the bottom of the paper.

Hennesey walked away. He had little doubt that the men in the rig who were now digging at the far end of the street were planting a similar notice. His fingers went automatically to his badge. As well toss it into the dust, he supposed, for whoever Donovan had elected as marshal it would not be himself.

As the morning passed, he found time dragged heavily and he was in the Silver Dollar almost before the swamper had finished brushing out. By that time he was fed up listening to the assurances of the dozens of men who promised to vote for him. Belle came to him the moment he entered the place. She met him without her usual smile.

'Well, Ed, at least we know now why Donovan was so set on buying up the town. He wants his own marshal. You'll stand against whoever he puts up, I suppose?'

'Oh sure, I'll stand all right. In fact I think most of the men in town will vote for me. I reckon it won't be as easy as all that though. Donovan will have some piece of skullduggery up his sleeve, you can bet on that.'

'Huh! I guess so, something with gunplay.'

'Wish I had chance to use my own gun – on Donovan.

That would settle things,' Hennesey said bitterly.

Carter came towards them, yawning and stretching as he usually did if he rose before ten in the morning. 'What's that about using a gun on Donovan? Sounds like a damn good idea.'

'Yeah, but it's only an idea,' Hennesey said, then gave him the details of the notice posted in front of Bohun's house.

Carter took the news phlegmatically enough. 'Well, it's no worse than we expected and there doesn't seem to be anything we can do to stop it. If we had a grain of sense between us we'd all three take the stage this afternoon and clear the hell out of this. As far as I can see we'll be cleared out sooner or later in any case.'

'Well, we haven't got that kind of sense,' Belle snapped. 'In any case we still own the saloon and I don't reckon we'll be selling that to Donovan.'

Carter shrugged. 'I can think of several things that Donovan might do that would make us glad to sell to him.'

'Donovan, Donovan. To hell with Donovan,' Belle shouted. 'Let's all have a drink before we go crazy.' She swung away towards the bar without waiting for an answer.

Carter and Hennesey were both about to follow her when the marshal's keen hearing brought to him the sound of hoofs. A great many hoofs. He went quickly to the batwings and took a sideways glance down the street. A pack of riders, between thirty and forty in number, were entering the street. He called the news to Carter then passed outside. Riders in such numbers could only come from the MD spread and he guessed they brought trouble of some sort. He stayed on the veranda until the pack of men and horses drew up. They seemed orderly enough as they climbed from their saddles and beat clouds of trail dust from their clothes before stamping into the saloon. Most of them called out a greeting of some kind as they passed him to line up in front of the bar. Their conduct there was peaceful enough too, if a trifle noisy, and after a few minutes of waiting, Hennesey moved off. He did not want to promote trouble by taking too much interest in the riders. He went as far as the livery and was talking to Moss when the sound of a voice raised in loud protest came to him. He turned just in time to see a man jostled from the boardwalk in front of the store and fall into the dust of the street.

'I guess I'd better see what's happening,' he said to Moss and walked slowly towards the group of men.

By the time he reached them the man in the street had picked himself up and was shouting loudly at three of Donovan's riders who now lounged indolently in front of the store.

One of them called back: 'You shouldn't crowd the boardwalk, feller. It's 'most bound to get you shoved out of the way.'

'You know darned well I wasn't doin' no crowdin',' the man in the street shouted back.

Hennesey stepped in front of the three on the boardwalk. 'What's it all about, fellers?'

The tallest of the three gave him an insolent look. 'The guy tried to push his way through us, so we pushed back. That's all.'

Hennesey looked at the three. 'Town's coming to something when a man who's near to sixty tries to push through three hard-bitten guys like you lot. Don't try any more of those tricks or you'll find yourself in the lockup.'

'That so? Well, I guess I'd be out again at twelve o'clock an' that ain't so darn far off.'

Hennesey turned away. 'Make sure you live to see it,' he flung over his shoulder.

He went to the man in the street. 'Better get along to your shack, Tom. I reckon there'll be more of this kind of business before long.'

'I'll be at that darned election,' Tom said angrily. 'Us needs a marshal to keep those MD coyotes in check.'

Hennesey had no sooner moved away than a gun began to crack and a man came hurtling down the middle of the street. Little spurts of dust close to his heels showed where the slugs were going. As the marshal came to the centre of the street the shooting ceased. He moved with long strides to the front of the saloon and spoke angrily to a puncher who was just holstering his gun.

'What in tarnation do you think you're up to?'

'Just a bit of fun, Marshal.'

'Well, lay off that kind of fun or you'll find yourself in real trouble.'

Hennesey's eyes went from the fun maker to the veranda of the saloon. Four of Donovan's men were in front of the batwings and one of the townsmen was coming up the steps. The four parted to give way for the man's entrance to the saloon then suddenly a foot was thrust forward and the man went sprawling. Hennesey took the three steps in a bound, grabbed at the shoulder of the puncher who had done the tripping up and drove a heavy punch to his jaw. As the man went reeling backwards the others grabbed for their guns, but the marshal's was out first. The three grinned at him and sauntered away. The one who had been punched glowered as if inclined to take the quarrel further then went after his companions. Hennesey holstered his gun and turned to the man who had been tripped.

'I guess you'll have to put up with what's just happened, Jake. Donovan's boys seem set on causing trouble.'

Jake grumbled a little and passed into the saloon. Hennesey, after a glance up and down the street, followed him. The saloon seemed unnaturally quiet. Ten, or a dozen, men were at the bar but there was little conversation going on and all seemed to be waiting on something, or someone.

Hennesey had a few words with Carter and Belle in which he told them what had happened in the street.

Carter looked uneasy. 'It sounds as if Donovan's men are set on scaring people off the street before election time.' He looked at his watch. 'Half an hour to go. Ed, I've a notion that us three will be riding that stage when it pulls out this afternoon.'

'The heck we will,' Belle snapped. 'At least, not unless someone hog-ties us and throws us into the coach.'

Hennesey gave a half grin and was about to make a reply when the steady banging of a sixgun sounded. He hurried to the batwings with Carter and Belle close on his heels. Thirty or so yards down the street Johnnie Callum was riding towards the saloon. He sat on the aged horse that he had taken from Manders in a manner that reminded Hennesey of a sack of wheat thrown carelessly across the saddle. Yet there was something in his way of riding that showed he was completely master of the horse. As the marshal watched, two slugs kicked dust from near to the hoofs of the animal but neither horse nor rider gave any sign of being affected by the shots. Hennesey's eyes went to the corner of the store from where the shots had been fired, and at the same time his hand went to the butt of his gun. Then he stopped the movement. The puncher who had been doing the firing had emptied his gun and was now making an attempt to reload. Johnnie's slowly moving horse had turned slightly and was going directly towards the gunman. Hennesey left the veranda at the same moment that Johnnie vaulted in an ungainly manner from the saddle. The new Colt was holstered at his waist but he made no attempt to draw the weapon although he must have seen that the Donovan man had nearly completed his loading. Hennesey drew in a deep breath and wondered if he should try to control the situation with his own gun, but even as the thought came to him he knew that the distance was too great for accurate shooting, if shooting was called for. Then something seemed to happen to Johnnie. His shambling, graceless striding became a quick whirl of arms and legs and the next moment the Donovan man was sprawling in the dust, his sixgun wrenched from him. He made a move to rise from the ground but was immediately flattened again by a swinging punch that had sledge hammer force in it. This time the man stayed down, or would have done if Johnnie's large hand had not gripped him by the bandanna and hauled him to his feet. The marshal came up at a run and shouldered his way between men who had got to the scene ahead of him. He was in time to see Johnnie shake the puncher like a child shakes a rag doll then with his free hand knock him senseless to the ground. In a moment the crowd of men, their loyalties always with the winner of a fist fight, surged forward to surround Johnnie, and Hennesey found himself shoved to one side by men demanding to buy Johnnie a drink. He got a quick glance at the boyish face. It was neither angry, excited or triumphant. Just solemn and a little uncertain. He had a feeling that Johnnie had come to town to see him, Hennesey, and began to push towards him again and as he did so a man shouted:

'Hey, fellers, here's the boss.'

The shouted words seemed to quell all excitement in the men, and Hennesey turned to see that Donovan, astride a big sorrel, was within a few feet of him. Donovan's glance went straight to himself.

'What's it all about, *Marshal?*'

The accent on the title was not lost on Hennesey but he answered quietly. 'One of your men trying to scare Johnnie Callum with gun shots.' He gestured over his shoulder. 'You can see how he got on.'

Donovan's eyes went to the still unconscious man then to

94

Johnnie and back to Hennesey.

'What did he lay him out with? The butt of a gun?'

'No, just with his fists.'

Donovan's eyebrows lifted. 'A useful fist. More useful at keeping order in my town than you are, Hennesey.'

Hennesey's face reddened. 'Maybe you didn't want the place keeping orderly.'

The beginnings of a grin curled Donovan's hard mouth. 'If that had been the case I wouldn't have called for the election of a marshal at all.' He pulled out a big watch. 'I make it a few minutes to noon. I take it you'll be at the meeting, Hennesey.'

Hennesey nodded. 'There isn't anything that would keep me away.'

Again Donovan gave his half grin. He turned a little in his saddle and boomed at the group of men.

'You have your instructions, boys. See that you carry them out. I want no disorder.'

Hennesey watched him ride towards the judge's house and his men troop after him. Those in the saloon were coming out too, he noticed. He glanced at Johnnie and saw the change that had come over his face. There was no doubt about the anger in it now. He said:

'What brought you to town, Johnnie?' and saw him start as if thought had been jerked from far away.

'Sam sent me to tell you that the fellers doing guard have gone back home. They got kind of restless sitting around and waiting. Sam says not to worry about it. He just thought you ought to know. What's this about a meeting?'

Hennesey explained what was afoot. 'Tell Sam and Lucy about it when you get back, will you?'

'Oh, sure, I'll tell them all right. Say, I thought a marshal's job was sort of permanent?'

Hennesey grinned. 'Walk with me to the meeting and

you'll see how permanent it is.'

'But all these people in town. The fellers that know you. They'll vote for you, won't they?'

'They might, if someone hasn't got a gun stuck in their ribs.'

'I get it,' Johnny said slowly. 'I get it. Donovan's going to try and crowd you out. Like the way he's done to homesteaders.'

Judge Bohun was already on his front porch when Hennesey and Johnnie reached the outskirts of the crowd. He had begun to speak, but stopped when he saw Hennesey, with Johnnie treading behind him, begin to push a way to the front. As the marshal got to the front rank he noted sourly that it consisted mainly of Donovan's men, most of them with their backs to the judge, their eyes on the town men.

Hennesey muttered: 'Stay here, Johnnie,' and moved across the clear space to Bohun's porch as the judge began again.

'Men, you all know why this meeting has been called. The ownership of most of the town has changed hands, and the new owner, Mr Donovan—'

Bohun faltered as Hennesey stepped alongside him, but at Hennesey's whispered, 'Carry on. I'm still marshal and I want to see that order is kept,' he continued:

'Mr Donovan has decided that the town ought to have a freely elected marshal. Now all you have to do is shout out your nominations, then step forward to back them up. I have to make it that you step forward so that I can make sure that outsiders, I mean men who do not belong to the district, do not shout out a nomination. As soon as I have all the nominations I shall put the names to a show of hands. Is that clear?'

A voice called out: 'Get on with it, Judge. We know how to vote, an' this ain't no election for a Senator.'

When the laugh had subsided another voice called: 'I nominate Ed Hennesey.'

Bohun's eyes appeared to range over the crowd of men. 'Will the gent who nominated Ed Hennesey step to the front?' There was a scuffle in the crowd but no one came forward. Bohun called out: 'Let the gent come forward, please.'

He waited a few seconds, got no response, then shouted: 'I guess the gent has changed his mind. Well, it's a free country. Anyone else care to nominate Ed Hennesey?'

This time there came a distinct howl of pain and as it died down, Hennesey brushed the judge to one side. He bawled out:

'Fellers, no more nominations for me. You'll only get hurt if you try. Let these Donovan fellers have their faked-up election and see what comes of it afterwards.' He might have said more, but the sight of Johnnie stepping into the clear space stopped him, and he heard the youngster's clearly shouted words with something like dismay.

'I'm nominatin' Ed Hennesey an' I'm out in front to show who I am.'

Hennesey saw half-a-dozen guns begin to slide from their holsters, then the judge cut in quickly:

'I'm much obliged, young feller and it's an example to the rest of the citizens, but I'm afraid it ain't hardly legal. I take it you don't claim to be twenty-one years of age, you haven't become a man yet?'

Johnnie shook his head. 'No, not yet, Judge, but I'm told if a feller owned a piece of land in the district he'd be entitled to nominate and vote.'

Bohun coughed. 'Why, yes, I guess that's so. If you have land and can prove that you own it that would entitle you to act as a grown man. Where is this land of yours and what's your title to it?'

Donovan suddenly appeared on the porch, having come, in spite of his height and bulk, almost unnoticed from indoors. He thundered out:

'What's this land you lay claim to, young Callum?'

'The land you stole from my Paw and Maw. A hundred and sixty acres alongside Chimney Rock. I drove my marker stakes in last night.'

Purple mounted from Donovan's collar to his ears. 'You drove marker stakes in my range. You young pup! If you were a man's age I'd have a rope round your neck in less than five minutes. Get to hell from here before I have you dragged out at the tail of a horse.'

Johnnie stood unmoved except that his gaze shifted to meet that of the judge. He said in an easy tone:

'Mister, is my nomination OK?'

Hesitation showed in Bohun's fat face, then he said carefully: 'Well, you see, son, Mr Donovan is disputing your title so I'm afraid—'

A shouted uproar drowned the rest of what the judge had to say. A gun banged and all in a moment the space in front of the judge's house was filled with fighting men. Three men made a concerted rush at Johnnie and he reeled under the first impact. Then, his long arms were flailing heavy punches and one of his attackers went down. A second grabbed him from the back in a neck hold whilst the third lowered his head to butt at Johnnie's middle. He met the head-down charge by lifting both feet from the ground and driving them at the man. The result was to bring the three of them down in a heap and break the neck hold on Johnnie. He heaved mightily at the weight on top of him and came bounding to his feet. He caught a glimpse of the blood-spattered face of the man he had driven his boots at, then saw the one who had had him by the neck was striving to come to his feet and drag out his gun at the same time. He remembered his own, hardly used Colt and made a snatch at the weapon, but his unpractised draw was clumsy and the weapon had not cleared leather when the other man fired. The slug seared across his hip, and with a yell of pain and rage he loosed his hold on the Colt and dived with wide stretched arms just as the hammer of the other's gun was falling for a second time. He felt the blast of the gun, and the roar of it in his ears deafened him, but he had his long arms round his adversary and whirled him clear of the ground before smashing him down. With this third man down he began to see the larger perspective of the battle. The dozens of men locked in struggles or standing clear of one another while they traded heavy punches. He saw Bohun backed against his own front door, his face chalk-white with fear, Donovan booming orders unheeded, and mostly unheard, then Hennesey moving swiftly about using his clubbed six-gun with discrimination. Then, a wave of brawling men dashed against him and he was in the fight again, but coolly, this time, and with the Colt in his hand, fending off mistaken townsmen who scarcely knew who they fought, while the long barrel of the Colt rapped hard against the head of any Donovan rider who came within range. At times, Johnnie found himself hard pressed, and he scarcely noticed the number of savage blows and kicks he received. At others he seemed almost alone and fighting with a single adversary. The battle moved up and down the street like a flowing and ebbing tide, first up against the livery, then with a sudden surge it moved a hundred yards to the front of the saloon where whistling and stamping from the frightened horses added to the din. Guns began to crack and the fighters divided sharply, Hennesey and Johnnie and forty or so townsmen backing to the Silver Dollar, whilst the sombreros of fifteen to twenty of Donovan's riders showed mostly near the judge's house. Thirty or so men were sprawled in the street or else making feeble attempts to get to their feet.

It seemed to Johnnie that the battle was as good as over, with his own side being the winners, until he noticed Hennesey moving rapidly about among the townsmen looking as if he were discussing with one, arguing with another. Johnnie got to his side and heard him say: 'I tell you, Seth, the fight's only just begun. Donovan will get his men organised then the shooting will really begin.'

'What do you reckon we ought to do then, Marshal?' Seth asked.

'The best we can do is throw two barricades across the street. One at each end of the saloon. That way we'll have most of their horses penned here. You know how most of these riders are on foot. Sort of half helpless. There's another thing too. The rifles are still in the saddle boots. We can raise a few rifles out of the saloon, maybe five or six, and that ought to hold them back.'

Seth moved away. 'I'll get the boys on that job right away, Ed. There's plenty will want to have a real go at pulling Donovan down to a natural size.'

Hennesey turned to Johnnie. 'I saw you putting in some pretty good work, feller. Heck, I didn't realize you were a real fighting man.'

Johnnie reddened. 'I didn't know I was going to start all this when I started yapping to Mr Donovan and that judge.'

Hennesey grinned. 'It had to start some time, Johnnie, and as it happened you picked the best time. Donovan had his men so set on just keeping the town fellers quiet and not daring to vote that he had them scattered too widely in the crowd to use their guns properly. Go see if you can grab yourself a drink from Belle or Luke. This fighting is thirsty work and there'll be plenty more to come.'

Belle appeared on the veranda as Johnnie was climbing the steps. There was a sparkle in her green eyes and she had a Winchester in the crook of her arm. She greeted him with:

'Hiya, fighting man. I was at the back of that crowd when you started to talk to the judge. Feller, you certainly sparked off one hell of a row when you asked that innocent question of yours. You want to get a bit handier with that Colt, though. Fists don't always win out.' Johnnie felt he wanted to apologise for starting the trouble but Belle rattled on. 'This idea of Ed's, throwing a barricade up on each side of the saloon is a darned good one. It means we've got most of the Donovan horses, nearly all, I should guess, and the rifles that go with them. Rifles are going to be the thing that counts.' She stopped short. 'My gosh, I'd forgotten. That store of Carlen's will have a dozen or more in it.' She began to shout. 'Ed, Ed. Carlen's store. What about the rifles in there?'

Hennesey came towards her with a worried look on his face. 'Tarnation, Belle. I'd forgotten all about the store. Donovan won't, you can bet. This is bad, Belle. The town men are full of fight at the moment but if they get ten or twelve rifles popping at them, it'll be a different story. How many can we raise?'

'Five and two shot-guns. Damnation, there's those in your office as well.'

'Six,' Hennesey said grimly, 'and it won't take long to break open the door. Hell, if we could only get a couple of men into that store first. They could maybe hold the store and cover my office at the same time. Be death to walk down that street now though.'

Johnnie's eyes had been going from one to the other and as Hennesey stopped speaking he said with quiet assurance:

'I reckon I could get up to that store if I had a horse that'll walk sort of easy.'

Hennesey looked at him, then his gaze travelled the hundred and fifty yards to where, in front of the judge's house, the Donovan men were now grouped. He could see

101

five men stretched in the dust and reckoned each of them to be dead. He said slowly:

'Be a mighty fine thing if you could do that, Johnnie, but I guess we wouldn't like to see you lying like those other fellers.'

Johnnie nodded solemnly. 'I wouldn't like it myself, Marshal, but I reckon it's important for someone to reach that store before Donovan's men do.'

'Let's find him the sort of horse he wants,' Belle said. 'I always knew that pulling Donovan down would be a sort of one-man job. I'm betting Johnnie is the guy for the chore.'

CHAPTER NINE

Ginity, who drove the stage said, after he had passed through the newly named Donovan City that, in all his years of handling the lines of freight and stage teams he had never seen anything like it. He tried to compare it with the times he had been attacked by Indians, or the occasions when road-agents had held him up, but found nothing equal. To come into a town that was engaged in a shooting war was, in itself, unusual. But to have the war cease and the street barriers opened while he changed horses before again taking the trail was something he would not easily forget. It was the surprise in the man, and the fact that he had only an equally surprised gun-guard to tell it to, that made him haul on the lines and set the drag the moment he sighted Sam and Lucy Stevens. Ginity told his story between spurts of tobacco juice, had it confirmed by his gun-guard, and after affirming that he had 'never in his dog-gone life seen anything to equal it,' drove on.

Sam looked at Lucy. 'That puts an end to looking for strays, Luce. I hate to ask you to go back home and stay on your own, but Hennesey will need all the help he can get.'

Lucy's mouth set mutinously. 'I agree that Ed will need help, but I'm coming with you. I'm handy enough with a rifle. Anyway, suppose Donovan wins out in the town, how long will it be before he comes to us again?'

Sam argued with her but he was not convinced of his own arguments. 'All right,' he finally agreed, 'we'll see how close we can get before someone throws lead at us.'

They were two miles from the town when Lucy said: 'Sam, we could leave the trail and get on to that red bluff that overlooks the town. It's too far off for shooting but with our spy glasses we might get an idea of what's going on.'

'Sure, better than riding in blind.'

From the two hundred feet high bluff they got a long view of the street with the saloon and its outside barriers at the distant end. Use of the glasses brought the details into sharp focus. Donovan and Bohun in front of the judge's house, men at the angle of shacks that were closer to the Silver Dollar, the tiny puffs of smoke as a gun was fired, more smoke puffs from behind a barrier, men that lay in the street without moving, and a riderless horse that seemed unaffected by the gunfire as it wandered about some yards from the barrier. Sam noted the peculiar wanderings of the horse, made little of it and said so to Lucy. She studied it for a minute then said:

'Well, it's a peculiar way for anyone to leave a horse. I can see its bridle all right and it looks, from the way that saddle blanket's hanging, that someone was either saddling or unsaddling. Who would be doing either in the middle of a gunfight?'

'Maybe someone who was trying to get it away. I don't think we can be any use up here, Luce. How'd it be if we try to get lower down and opposite the judge's house? We might get a shot or two that would surprise Donovan's crowd.'

'Yes, we'll try that. I feel it's odd about that horse, though.'

Donovan had seen the horse also but the only thing it brought to his mind was the fact that his own men's horses were behind the barricade Hennesey had had erected. Not being able to have the use of the horses was bad enough, but not having the use of the rifles that were in the saddle boots was worse. With them, he felt, his men would soon sweep a clear way to the saloon and put an end to the fighting, but without them the Donovan riders were compelled to the use of sixguns fired from as close as they dared get to the barricade. And each time a man tried to shorten that distance the rifles of one or other of the defenders picked him off. In the last quarter of an hour four of Donovan's men had gone down that way. It was Bohun who remembered that the store had a stock of rifles and as soon as he mentioned it, Donovan cursed him for not thinking of the store earlier on.

Donovan measured the distance to the store with his eye. Half way to the barrier, which meant that a good rifle shot would get anyone approaching it. Nevertheless, with sufficient caution, it should be possible for men to get there. He called the puncher nearest to him and put the proposition to the man.

'A month's pay if you can make it, and that goes for anyone else with you.'

The puncher grinned at him and moved away. A few minutes later, Donovan saw him and two other men begin a cautious advance from shack to shack towards the store. Three or four minutes later the sharp eyes of Belle picked up the movement. She called Hennesey's attention and both of them tried to get one or the other of Donovan's men in their rifle sights, but the erratic movements of the apparently wandering horse blocked the chance of a shot. Their eyes went to the horse again with its saddle blanket trailing halfway to the ground. The hunched up figure of Johnnie, under the horse's belly and clinging to a rope that was fast around the animal's middle, was quite plain to them, and they wondered just how long it would be before Donovan or one of his men would see the deception and train their sixguns on the horse. There had been little shooting for the past ten minutes and they put that down to Donovan trying to get time for his men to reach the store.

Hennesey said, to break the strained silence behind the barricade: 'There's one thing, Belle. That horse of yours ain't gun shy.'

She laughed brittley. 'Gun shy ! That old crittur's as deaf as a post and wouldn't shie at anything less than a wagon load of gunpowder. Don't know what I keep him for 'cept that I've had him since heck knows when.'

'Well, I'm thankful you didn't let him go for the price of his hide. Which is what I would have done,' Carter said.

Johnnie too, in his cramped position, was thankful for the horse's age and complete indifference to the shooting that had been lively enough when he had first sent the horse moving from a side alley near to the Silver Dollar. The only thing bad about this horse, so far as he was concerned, was that, besides being indifferent to gunfire it had almost the same disregard to his gentle tugs on the reins and his fiercely growled instructions to get on. He could see the store now, to his left about twenty yards ahead, and the temptation to drop to the ground and then make a dash for the place was great. Particularly as he, too, had noticed the almost complete absence of shooting. But he remembered that he had to do more than reach the store. There would be the business of bursting a way in, for the place would certainly be barred. He growled threats at the horse and tugged on the left rein as the animal showed a strong tendency to veer to the right. The result was a complete stop. He used up his small stock of adjectives then slewed his head round to the racketing of sixguns. Two men, their bodies flattened against the side of the store were pumping slugs into the lock of the door. He dropped to the ground, rolled from under the horse and came to his feet, grabbing at the Colt as he did so. Somehow, the weapon came cleanly from its holster and firmly into his grip as he took his first striding leap towards the store. He loosed a shot, feeling the exhilarating buck of the .45 against his wrist. The shot went closer to the two men than he had a right to hope for and both turned to face him. The gun of one belched flame but the hammer of the other's weapon came down ineffectively. A third man came running across the width of the street towards him, firing as he ran. Johnnie turned the Colt in his direction but before he could press the trigger the man was down from a rifle shot. Johnnie swung his gun towards the pair in front of the store, triggered off two shots and saw them break away at a run. He had a fleeting realization that both their guns must be empty, then he was against the door of the store. He shoulder-charged the door and rebounded with a hail of long-range six-gun shots peppering all about him. He bounced the door again, using all the weight of his body, and heard it creak under the impact. A third charge sent him floundering into the dim interior. He used a moment or two to get his bearings then heaved the door shut on its crippled hinges and began to pile dry goods boxes against it. In less than three minutes he had the door effectively blocked and had located fifteen well-oiled rifles racked behind the counter. He chose a Springfield, and after a few seconds of hunting about found shells for it. He wiped away the surplus oil, loaded the weapon, then looked about for the best place to use it from. A shuttered window gave on to the street but was useless from the point of directing fire against Donovan and his men. Perhaps he ought not to follow the marshal's idea after all, but take an axe and smash all the stocks of the rifles, then make a run across to Hennesey's office and do the same with the rifles and shot-guns there. There would not be much risk in a sudden dart across the street. Those behind the barricade would not be expecting it and the range for Donovan's sixguns was too great. He felt the smooth, brown stock of the Springfield and was aware that he could not take an axe to this or any other of the dully gleaming weapons in the place. The thought of the axe gave him an idea and he looked hopefully at the low roof over his head. Like the roof of most buildings in the town, it was boarded, near flat and would, he guessed, have an outside covering of rusting sheet iron. He put the rifle down and picked up a tree-felling axe. From the top of the counter he swung the axe upwards at the roof. Long swinging blows, each of which sent the keen bite of the axe deeply into the wood and part way through the iron covering. It took him ten sweating minutes to carve a jagged hole big enough for his body, a few minutes more to pass through it and on to the roof every rifle and shotgun he could see in the place. Then he was on the roof himself in the baking afternoon sunshine, with enough weapons and ammunition to equip a small army. Three others of the rifles proved to be Springfields and he loaded them also, then eyed the men between himself and the judge's house, across the street and sixty yards distant. He saw two men skulking at the side of a shack, one of them rolling a smoke whilst the other kept some kind of a watch. The range was not more than twenty-five yards and a rifle in the hands of a man more experienced that Johnnie would have killed the pair of them. Johnnie sighted carefully on the lookout, squeezed the trigger and then gave a grunt of anger as a chip of woodwork flew from above the man's head. The pair vanished from his sight and he turned his gaze towards the judge's shack. A few men were moving about but after his last experience he knew that they were too difficult a target for himself. He considered firing in the hope of scaring them into running, then Donovan himself appeared in the doorway of the house. He looked, even at that distance, huge, all powerful, even to the extent of being something more than an ordinary man. Johnnie's anger rose as he thought of the way Donovan was using his friends. He stoked his anger further by calling to mind that this was the man who had swept his parents from their home, had perhaps had them killed. He put the rifle to his shoulder and got Donovan in the vee. This time, Johnnie told himself, he would not miss. He thought of every instruction Lucy had given him, even to the holding of his breath at the moment of pulling the trigger. The explosion came and Donovan staggered a little, then clapped his right hand on his left shoulder. Johnnie swore, using words that were strange to his mouth. His anger rose to a red rage and he pumped shells from the rifle until it was emptied, then grabbing up a second gun sent its lead singing towards the judge's house. Men scattered in all directions as Johnnie emptied the second gun and began to trigger the third, then suddenly the mist of his rage cleared and he saw the street was empty of Donovan's men. Cold anger supplanted the passionage rage, anger at himself for having missed such an opportunity for putting an end to Donovan. Clumsily, but methodically, he reloaded both his own Colt and a Springfield then dropped with them to the floor of the shop. He tore down his barricade and wrenched open the door. He reached the middle of the street and found it as clear of life as a salt desert. He walked towards Bohun's house with long strides, the rifle held ready to throw to his shoulder. He made twenty paces before the door of the judge's house opened again and for a brief moment showed the figure of the judge himself. Then the door of the house slammed loudly with Bohun on the inside. Johnnie knew instinctively that Donovan also was in the house, had probably gone there to have his wound bandaged. He strode on until he was in front of the house and not more than ten paces from it, then he raised his voice.

'Come out, Donovan. I'm waiting for you.'

A window at the side of the door crashed and a .45 slug clipped a hole through Johnnie's hat. He threw the rifle inexpertly to his shoulder and pumped two shots through the space where the glass had been. Bad though his shooting was, he was calm enough in the silence that followed to know that Donovan, or whoever else had fired the single shot at him, was no longer in the room. He advanced without fear and had one leg through the broken window when something made him glance down the street. A horse, with Donovan in the saddle, broke from a side opening and picked up to a gallop as it reached the street. Johnnie dragged his leg back again and cleared from the porch in a bound. He put the rifle to his shoulder and sent slug after slug whining after the big rancher until the weapon was empty, then with a grunt of disappointment at having missed repeatedly he lowered the weapon and went again to Bohun's house. He entered through the window, searched the house but the judge seemed to have left the place at the same time as Donovan. Johnnie came outside again, not sure in his own mind what he would have done with Bohun had he found him. He walked towards the barricaded Silver Dollar, thinking how easy it had been with a rifle to send Donovan and his men running. With his lack of experience at gun fighting, Johnnie failed to realize that the quick use of three rifles in succession had sounded to Donovan's men that at least four men were attacking them. Being themselves without rifles even Donovan's authority had not persuaded them against running.

Men were climbing over the barrels, boxes and cases that made the barricade when he got within a few yards of it. A cheering, boisterous mob who were convinced that Donovan had been finally pulled to earth and that Johnnie was the man who had done the pulling. It was minutes before he could rid himself of the back-slapping, hand-wringing crowd and get to where Hennesey, Carter and Belle were standing. He got unstinted praise from the three plus a lecture from Hennesey on the foolhardiness of walking down the middle of the street with a rifle in his hand. Johnnie took it all, grinning a little, then said:

110

'I'll have to put in a lot of practice with a rifle and six-gun. I ought to have got that Donovan when he was on the run.'

Belle's eyebrows lifted a little. 'You mean to say you were trying to hit the guy?'

'Of course. What else would I shoot for?'

'I'll leave it to you to explain, Ed,' Belle said helplessly. 'Although personally I'm in favour of shooting Donovan no matter what angle the slug comes from.'

Hennesey coughed. 'It's more than a feller can explain in much less than a lifetime, Johnnie, but we don't reckon to shoot a guy in the back. And if he takes it on the run we reckons to let him go. It's a sort of, well, you know when two kids are fighting and one of them hollers "enough"?'

Johnnie shook his head. 'I never fought with any other kids. Never got to know any, least not as far as I can remember. I sort of thought that if a feller shot at you, he must want to kill you and the best thing to do was to shoot back and kill him as soon as you could.' He looked at Hennesey woodenly. 'I still think it's the best thing to do.'

Hennesey sighed. 'You could be right, Johnnie. I'll teach you all I know about gunthrowing. I'm not the best but I'm pretty good.'

Belle laughed. 'I reckoned you'd find it awkward, Ed. What are we going to do about these horses of Donovan's – corral them somewhere until Donovan gets around to sending men for them? There's near to forty and that's quite a bunch to find feed for.'

'We'll get some in the livery and scatter the rest around somehow,' Hennesey said.

'You mean, you'll let Donovan take those horses back?' Johnnie said in a puzzled tone.

Hennesey smiled. 'Stealing a man's horse is a crime, Johnnie, even if the man has done something bad to you.'

Misery twisted Johnnie's face and for a few moments he

111

stood silent, scuffing the dust of the street with one foot. Then he gave Hennesey a direct look.

'I'm not going to hide what I've done any longer, you and the other folks around here have been too good to me. You all sort of think I'm better than I am. Marshal, I killed a man then went off with his horse.'

Belle drew in her breath sharply. 'Well, of all the things. Johnnie, what do you want to go shooting your head off like that for?'

Carter scratched the side of his head. 'Just who have you killed, Johnnie? It couldn't have been any one around here or we'd have heard about it.'

'Best tell me all about it, Johnnie,' Hennesey said.

'It was that Josh Manders,' Johnnie began, then poured out the whole story as he knew it.

The three listened in silence, then Hennesey asked a few questions. He pondered long on Johnnie's answers then said:

'It comes to this, Johnnie. Manders practically kidnapped you, there was no reason why he couldn't have brought you in to a town, this one for instance. From then on he used you as a slave. You would have had a perfect right to kill him and make your escape the best way you could. However, I don't think you did kill him.'

'How do you figure that out?' Belle put in quickly.

Hennesey grinned. 'Sheep. The place that Johnnie describes as being where he had the fight with Manders isn't more than thirty miles away and without someone to herd them they'd have been all over the territory and you can bet we'd have learned about that quickly enough.'

'But I was three days getting to this town,' Johnnie protested. 'I wouldn't take three days to cover thirty miles.'

'You went without any sense of direction. That's all. You could have taken a week to cover the distance. No, Johnnie, I'm not arresting you on any murder charge. As for that crowbait you call a horse. Let's say you borrowed it for a spell.'

The wide smile came back to Johnnie's face. 'Gosh, that's good to know, Marshal. I wasn't sort of afraid of being caught and hung but I'd got to like it a powerful lot with Sam and Lucy and—'

'And you wanted to hang on to what you'd got,' Carter put in. 'It's the same with us, except that we've got more to hang on to.'

'I've got my land,' Johnnie said solemnly, 'an' I'm going to get around to making it the best homestead in the district. I'll make a start as soon as Sam can spare me.'

Belle stared at him with wonder in her eyes. 'You'll make a start. What about Donovan? And talking about Sam and Lucy, they're coming this way now.'

The others turned and saw the Stevenses coming through the crowd of men who still lingered. Lucy slipped from her saddle.

'Johnnie, you were great, just great. Sam and I had gotten to a place where we hoped to do some good with our rifles and we saw the whole thing. My land! Donovan of all men on the run. Lordie! he'll never forget that.'

Johnnie grinned then saw the shine in Lucy's eyes and colour mounted up the back of his neck. 'The marshal said I was a plumb fool for coming up the middle of the street to go after Donovan. I guess I was.'

'Let's all get something to eat,' Belle said, turning towards the saloon. 'I guess we're all plenty hungry and we can talk about Donovan's next move while we chow.'

Lucy and Johnnie were the last pair to go up the steps of the veranda and he turned as he felt her hand on his arm. Again he coloured at the glow in her eyes then blood surged to his head as she said with quiet emphasis:

'Johnnie, you were no fool. You're just great.'

CHAPTER TEN

Defeat. The word was acid in Donovan's mind, corroding his thinking power until the setback he had received in town magnified itself to the size of a major loss. Never, not even in the days when he had first set foot in this land and done battle with marauding Indians, had he been licked. Indians, small-time ranchers and homesteaders had all turned and ran before his ruthless methods. There had been one exception, Brett Stevens. Brett had held out against him with formidable courage and in the end died a natural death and left Sam and Lucy to carry on.

He had used every method short of actual violence to push the pair from their land but at last turned to it again because the need for their range, with its valuable access to water, grew greater as his own herd reached vaster proportions. It had got so that, besides coveting the land he was almost desperately in need of it. And now he was defeated, licked and mainly because of the action of an ignorant, overgrown youth. What in a hell had made him run from the kid? It could not be that he had been infected with Bohun's fear, for the judge had struggled out through a back window the moment the kid had yelled for himself to come into the street. No, it could not have been the judge's influence, for he remembered calmly smashing a front window and sighting his sixgun on to young Callum. He had done all that calmly enough and yet he had missed at ten or a dozen paces. Also, he had fired no second shot in answer to Callum's wildly fired slugs. No, he had stood for a moment as if some paralysis had his limbs and then fled as if he had never before faced gunfire. Was it that he was getting old? Were hand and eye no longer to be relied on when it came to gunplay? He had a notion that his disgruntled range hands were talking that way about him even though he had been no further than the front porch of the house this last three days. Stone, in his necessary comings and goings to the house, had somehow conveyed the idea to his mind although the only words the foreman had spoken that made any reference to the subject were threats of what he would do to young Callum the moment his own wrist was sufficiently mended. Donovan wrestled with his mental as well as physical defeat until the fourth morning after the affair in town, then he ordered his horse to be saddled.

He rode alone and the thing uppermost in his mind was the necessity for finding out whether or not he was still the man he had reckoned himself to be or an ageing coward who had run before a younger and more virile man. He purposed to do this simply by finding young Callum and forcing him into a close range shooting match. After that, and here his mind was not quite so certain of itself, he might try the same tactics on Sam Stevens. He deliberately forced himself to ride via the way of the town although commonsense indicated that being alone he was liable to receive a slug in the back from some vengeful townsman and passed through without other incident than a good deal of staring from those who saw him go.

Mid morning brought him close to the Stevens' house without having seen any of its occupants and he reached almost to the veranda before Lucy's voice called:

'Far enough, Donovan. Rein right there unless you want a slug through you.'

Donovan reined in and endeavoured to make out Lucy's shadowed figure more clearly, but the glare of the sun defeated him.

'Sam at home?' he called.

'Doesn't matter to you where he is. You've got a nerve coming here. There isn't anything you want to say to him that you can't say to me, so say it and get out of here.'

'If you're all alone you'd best not take that tone with me.'

'I am all alone, go for your gun if you want to. I'd just as soon finish the business here and now.'

Donovan laughed. 'You always did have plenty of sand for a girl, Lucy, but this is a game for men. I wouldn't have minded a talk with Sam, but young Callum is my main objective.'

'Well, he's not here, so—' Lucy stopped suddenly.

Donovan laughed again. 'That's about all I want to know. The young pup's away at that precious piece of land he's staked out. I thought he might be but it was quicker to ride here and find out than to go all that way and draw a blank. You can put your gun down. I'm on my way to see Johnnie Callum.'

As he turned his mount he came nearer to getting a shot in his back than he had ever been in his life. Lucy's finger quivered on the trigger as several things struck her at once. Sam was miles away down by the river. Johnnie had gone to have yet another stare around at his piece of land as Donovan had so rightly guessed. Why hadn't she told him he was out on the range? That would have given her time to go and warn Johnnie. For she knew now that if anything happened to Johnnie, life, for her, would be an empty thing. It had taken this visit of Donovan to make her see that clearly.

She watched Donovan's fast receding figure and her

thoughts went ahead of him. He would come to Johnnie under the cover of the great rock chimney and be upon him, gun in hand, before Johnnie was aware of his arrival. And there seemed nothing she could do to prevent it. She knew so well what would be in Donovan's mind. Johnnie had made him turn and run. Now, the rancher would take vengeance by shooting him down from some convenient cover. On a sudden decision she flew across to the horse barn, and although she realized that pursuit of Donovan was hopeless she struggled frantically to throw on a saddle and bridle a fast mare. In less than ten minutes she was out of the barn, the rifle across her knees, as she kicked the mare to its best pace. Donovan was a mere speck in the distance and remained that way in spite of her desperate efforts to close on him. In the rough ground that surrounded the chimney she lost sight of him altogether and was near to tears in her uncertainty as to the exact location of Johnnie's patch of land. Then she heard a sixgun shot, distant but quite distinct, and she turned her mount towards the sound. There were five more shots and they filled her with hope. Johnnie must have seen Donovan, after all, and if he had acquired a little skill with his Colt he would have some kind of chance of fighting back. Her grip tightened on both rifle and reins. Donovan could look for no fair play from her. A shot in the back was his if she got a chance.

But the shots that Lucy heard were all from Johnnie's own gun. Donovan was just rounding a boulder when he, too, heard them. He saw Johnnie aim and fire at a stone on the ground. The stone jumped high in the air. The same thing happened again, and Donovan knew that he was no longer dealing with a mere youth who could not use a gun. Johnny was thumbing fresh shells into the Colt as Donovan slid from the saddle and walked towards him. The shells were going into the gun slowly and awkwardly. Donovan was about thirty yards away and reckoned to make the distance twenty by the time the gun was loaded. He guessed the Colt would be holstered then drawn again for further practice and he intended to call Johnnie while the gun was still holstered. The fact that he reckoned easily to beat Callum to a draw only added zest to the killing. By all range laws it would be a fair fight. Moving soft footed in spite of his giant bulk, Donovan passed one of Johnnie's marker stakes and smiled cynically as he saw the scrawled notice fastened to the stake. He made five more yards. Callum had completed the loading and was about to slide the Colt into its holster. The slight wound on Donovan's left shoulder burned a little adding further to his desire to see this youngster dead. His hand went to the butt of his gun and at that moment Johnnie turned. Donovan drew, levelled and fired with practised speed, but his slug went wide. Johnnie's move was slow and dragging by comparison, the roar of his Colt being measurably behind Donovan's but the more accurate shot clipped the brim of the rancher's hat and sent his second shot even wider than the first. In a rage at his failure he tried to steady himself for a third shot and had Johnnie sighted when the Colt roared again and the slug from it ripped the weapon from his hand. For a moment, Donovan knew the fear of death, then he saw that Callum had lowered the Colt and was walking towards him. Johnnie's words came slowly.

'Get off my land and stay off. If I see you here again I'll kill you. I'd do it now only I've been listening to some talk about fair play. Don't reckon to understand it properly but I'm giving it a trial.'

Donovan gaped surprise. 'You're a damned fool, Callum. You've had luck, that's all. Take my advice and don't play it too hard.'

'You'd better get moving,' Johnnie said quietly.

Donovan shrugged. 'No hurry for me, seeing that you're

so high minded about fair play.' He took a side glance and saw the still distant figure of Lucy coming towards them. 'A pity your woman friend couldn't have seen that clever shot of yours. She'd have appreciated it.'

'Woman friend! I don't have any woman friend. At least—'

Johnnie stopped speaking and a dark flush of anger coloured his face at the barely understood innuendo. 'If you're talking about Lucy Stevens—'

'Who else? But I'd better shut up, you've got a gun,' Donovan grinned.

Knowledge came to Johnnie. He had licked this man in a gun battle. Not by accident but because he had learned to take his time. Now the big man was trying to taunt him into putting down the gun and carrying on the fight in a hand-to-hand struggle. Donovan was banking on his six extra inches of height and his forty or fifty pounds of superior weight. Well, he could have the fight that way if he wished it. He grinned back at Donovan.

'I beat your foreman into the dust without having any gun and I can do the same to you. In fact I can lick you so as they'll have to bring a rig to take you home. I'm holstering the gun and then I'm taking the belt off. You can either start running for your horse or stay and fight it out.'

Donovan made no answer but his eyes glinted as he saw the Colt slide into its holster and Johnnie's hands engage with the broad buckle of the belt. He waited until the buckle was loose then moved forward with speed. There was no wildness about his arm movements and no clumsiness in his footwork and his first blow rocked Johnnie on his heels. The second sent him reeling off balance and down to earth. Donovan followed quickly and drove his boot at Johnnie's head, the one form of attack that Manders' treatment had made him skilled in avoiding. He rolled to the kick, seized the booted foot and with a quick twist of his long arms threw

Donovan to the ground. He was up in a moment and flung himself on top of the rancher, intent on securing a throat hold. Donovan met his downwards dive with the soles of both boots driven hard into Johnnie's middle. Johnnie's breath departed in a whoosh of sound and he landed yards away on the flat of his back. Donovan came agilely to his feet, saw the gun-belt some yards from him and charged towards it. Johnnie saw his danger and, gulping for air, got somehow to his feet. He reeled on unsteady legs towards the rancher and his hands clamped on the other's wrists. Donovan, with the Colt in his hand, tried to twist from the grip but found himself in a hold that he could not shake. Next he put all his strength into turning the Colt against Johnnie's body whilst his hate filled eyes glared into the face of a man who, although gasping painfully for breath, was still grinning. For some seconds the pair remained almost motionless, standing toe to toe with barely an inch between their heaving chests while the arm muscles of both cracked audibly under the strain that was upon them. Then the Colt that was in Donovan's grip began to turn outwards, the muzzle of it vibrating slightly in the rancher's fierce hold. Johnnie's grin widened as he felt Donovan give slightly and he braced himself to a still greater effort. The rancher felt pain shooting from his wrists to his shoulders and under the inexorable, twisting pressure, his arms began to spread, the fingers open, until with a thud the Colt dropped to the ground. It was the rancher's breath that was now coming gustily and realizing the fact, Johnnie gave a great upwards heave to the man's arms that pulled him off balance. He had Donovan in a position to throw him to the ground when the sound of hoofs made him jerk his head round. In the split second that he was relaxed, Donovan broke free and made a dive for the Colt. Johnnie had a blurred vision of two things happening at once as he went after Donovan. Lucy, a rifle in her hand, scrambling from the saddle and Donovan with the gun again in his possession. He grappled Donovan as the Colt exploded deafeningly, wrenched the weapon from him as if his grasp had been a child's, then slammed him full in the face with the barrel of it. Donovan became suddenly inert and Johnnie came to his feet to see Lucy stretched on the ground. He saw, even as he bounded towards her, the blood that was flowing down the side of her face and he let out a cry that was almost one of a madman. A second later he was calm enough. The wound just above Lucy's temple might or might not be a serious one, but the only thing he could do was work on staunching the flow of blood then get her to where she could get better attention. The town was nearer than her own home, he decided.

The full heat of the afternoon sun was blistering the street when he came to it and Lucy, on the saddle in front of him, might be dead for all that he knew. She had stirred slightly when he had mounted her and himself on Donovan's big roan, which he had taken as better able to bear the double weight, but since then his anxious, downward glances had shown him no sign of life in her. Running and shouting men had carried the news of his arrival to the saloon before he himself got there and both Hennesey and Carter were waiting to take the girl from him. She was carried quickly inside and upstairs and then the bedroom door was closed with Belle and one of the townswomen inside the room. Johnnie trooped down the stairs with Carter and Hennesey. He answered their questions with monosyllables, heard Carter say that he would get someone to ride out and let Sam know what had happened whilst all the time his mind was busy with two questions.

Would Lucy live? and how soon could he get after Donovan and settle him for ever?

It was an hour before Belle came downstairs and the

121

gravity of her face quenched the little hope that had been dwelling in Johnnie.

'Wound's not too bad in itself,' Belle said, 'but there's a kind of fever rising in her. That's got me plain scared.'

Johnnie grabbed her arm painfully. 'She'll live, won't she? She's just got to. Got to, I tell you.'

Belle made no attempt to shake off his hold, hurtful though it was. 'Johnnie, we'll all do our best for her, but a thirty mile ride in the hot sun is quite something on top of being shot.'

Johnnie released his hold on her arm. He gazed around the saloon as if his eyes did not comprehend what was before them, then in a few long strides he reached the bar.

'Gimme some of that whiskey stuff,' he said harshly.

'Whiskey, Johnnie?' the bartender said. 'It's bad drinking if you're not used to it.'

'Gimme, I say.'

Belle was at his side. She nodded to the bartender. 'One from my own bottle, Doone.'

Johnnie downed the drink in a gulp, spluttered a little, then looked at Belle.

'Feel any better now, Johnnie?'

'Some. I'm going after that skunk, Donovan.'

'Don't get yourself killed, Johnnie. If she gets better she'll want you and wanting hurts like hell. I guess you know that now.'

Johnnie gave a cracked laugh. 'I know it all right, Belle, but I'm not fooling myself that a girl like Lucy could ever want a feller like me. Least, not in the way I want her.'

Belle smiled. 'It's your name she been muttering since she's been in that bed, Johnnie, and a girl doesn't mutter a man's name unless she thinks a heck of a sight of him. You just be careful how you go.'

Johnnie nodded and strode swiftly out of the saloon.

Hennesey, who had been watching him, came to Belle's side.

'Where's he going to, Belle? Not after Donovan, I hope.'

'He's doing just that, Ed.'

'For hell's sake why didn't you call me? I'll never overtake him by the time I saddle up. That horse of Donovan's is real fast.'

Carter caught the gist of the conversation. 'There isn't anything you can do, Ed, if you do catch up. Johnnie's a man and he's gone to call Donovan to a showdown. You can't interfere with that. If I were you, I wouldn't want to.'

'Hell, Johnnie can't be always lucky,' Hennesey protested. 'Twice he's gone for Donovan and each time the luck has been on Johnnie's side. It won't last, I tell you, I'm going after him.'

'You try to stop Johnnie from doing what he wants to do and you'll have a fight on your hands,' Belle warned.

'Just the same, I'm going,' Hennesey said grimly.

Carter shrugged. 'I reckon I'll string along with you then.'

'You!' Hennesey's surprise was as great as Belle's.

'That's right. I can't shoot and I'm scared of fights, but if an eighteen year old kid can go after a man like Donovan then I guess I've just got to find enough guts to go along and watch.'

'Glory be,' Belle murmured. 'Glory be. This I never thought to see.'

CHAPTER ELEVEN

Donovan got unsteadily to his feet and passed his hand over his blood-caked jaw. He probed the ragged gash that the gun muzzle had made, winced at the pain of it, then in a shambling walk went down the steep descent to the river. Bathing his face made the raw wound sting and brought on an ache he had not noticed before. He stood for a few moments dabbing his face dry with his handkerchief then retraced his steps uphill. There was still some confusion in his mind about what had happened, but the sight of Lucy's mare grazing peacefully alongside the bony mount that belonged to Johnnie reawakened his memory. He remembered most strongly the shot he had fired and the girl's scream, so suddenly cut off as she had dropped to the ground. He wondered if she was dead and the possibility of it jolted him. If that was the case, would even he get away with it? Then he jerked his shoulders back. Get away with it? Of course he could. It was his town, just the same as this patch of land with its ruined soddy, half buried in thorn and weeds was his. He must be feeling his age to think otherwise. He went over to the mare and was about to mount when he recalled that he was without his gun. He searched around a little, found the weapon, checked that it was undamaged, saw to the loading, then climbed on to the mare's saddle. The smallness of the horse after his own giant of a mount angered him and he had a feeling that he looked slightly ridiculous. He would look more than ridiculous if he allowed the full story of the recent incident to reach the town and eventually his own range hands. He looked at his watch, apparently he had been stretched unconscious for nearly half a hour. Callum, with the girl, would be well on his way to the Stevens' ranch. No possibility of overtaking him on this small mare. On the other hand there was little possibility of himself being expected to follow to the place. With the smallest amount of luck he would settle with young Callum and Sam Stevens at the same time. Of course, there was the girl. She might be only wounded. Donovan's already grim mouth set in a harder line. A pity if she was not dead for he could not afford to leave her alive. Her tale would undoubtedly bring his prestige into the dust.

He followed much the same route that he had covered earlier and saw two things that would ordinarily have sent him into a wild rage. The first was a pair-horse wagon with a stained canvas tilt, undoubtedly that of a homesteader. The second, a distant view of grazing sheep. He noted both items but for the moment they were crowded from his mind by what he had in hand. He kept telling himself, as he rode, that he had to handle this business alone; had to do it that way so that he could go back to his ranch and let it be known that what a whole bunch of men had failed to do for him he had done for himself. Nearing the house he had so blown up his self esteem that he was working up a scheme to finish off Carter the moment he had done with young Callum and the Stevens' pair. However, he retained sense enough to rein in when he got within a long rifle shot of the place, to study his best approach to the house. There was low ground to the right of the house and it seemed to him that if he made his way to it he could probably come up to the barns unnoticed.

He moved in that direction and came to a dry gulch, steep-sided and narrow. He let the mare slither down one bank and was beginning to climb the other side when a voice called out.

'Donovan.'

He had no need to look up to know that the caller was Sam Stevens, and waited only for the bark of a shot or the order to draw. It would be one or the other whether the girl was dead or not, and Donovan began to curse himself for his foolhardiness in riding into a trap. Then Stevens' voice called again and he looked up to see Sam sitting his horse at the top of the bank.

'You're on my land, Donovan. I ought to kill you on sight but I guess murder ain't in my line. Better get moving and stay that way.'

Donovan mastered his surprise. It appeared that Callum had not taken the girl home, or at least, Stevens was not aware of it yet. He had the option of riding away and leaving Stevens to wonder what had brought him to the place or, if he could get to the side of Stevens, force a fight on him. He was on the point of deciding to leave when Sam whipped out his gun.

'Sit right where you are, Donovan, and start talking. I've just noticed that's Lucy's mare you're riding. Should have seen it before but she looks different from up here.'

Donovan's mouth went dry. Unless he could find some way of bluffing Sam, the chips were down for the last game.

'I'm waiting for an answer, Donovan,' Stevens said in a hard voice. 'You've got ten seconds to say how you come to be on that mare.'

'My own went lame,' Donovan blurted out. 'Almost in front of your house. I was calling on you to see if we couldn't fix things between us—'

'That sounds like a goddam lie, but go on.'

'There was no one at your place,' Donovan managed to put conviction into what he knew was true, 'so I borrowed the mare and set out to look for you. I reckoned you mightn't be far away.'

'And you picked Lucy's mare, the smallest horse of the bunch, or maybe you're going to tell me it was already saddled for you.'

Donovan seized on the chance. 'Odd though it sounds, that's the way it was. The mare was hitched to the veranda rail but I went through the house and all around and there was no sign of Lucy or young Callum.'

Filled with a number of suspicions he could not put a name to, Sam snapped out:

'I don't believe a darn word of what you've been saying. Throw down your gun and ride back to the house and go carefully.'

Glad of even this breathing space, Donovan let the gun drop to the ground and turned his mount about. He thought he could see the mistake he had made and there was a possibility he might still ride free if he did not delay. Lucy, he guessed, was not dead but badly wounded and Callum had taken her to town as being the nearest place. There had not yet been time for the news to reach Sam. Donovan began to calculate time as he guided his horse towards the house. Callum would have reached town by now, supposing that that was where he had gone. A message would undoubtedly be sent to Stevens and if it were done immediately the messenger should reach the Stevens' place in the next half hour. Could he, by any means, trick Sam Stevens into letting him go before that time? It would be difficult in the face of the fact that his own mount was not at the house. Suppose he failed to persuade Stevens into letting him go free. What then? A slug fired in anger or would Sam take him into town and hand him over to Hennesey?

Donovan felt his spine crawl at either prospect and as the house came into view he had the mad idea of jabbing spurs to the mare's flanks and trying to make a run for it. He half turned his head and saw from the grim expression in Sam's face that the cocked gun in his hand would blast immediately if any such move was made. A minute later Sam's voice came, harsh and dry, as if his throat were constricted.

'I don't see your horse, Donovan.'

'It could have wandered.'

'You said it was lame. Spit the truth out before I blast your spine in halves.'

Desperation prompted Donovan's inventive powers. He pulled the mare to a standstill and twisted in the saddle to face Stevens.

'All right, I'll give it you straight. I was over on that patch of land near Chimney Rock. The piece young Callum reckons is his. We got to pulling guns then Lucy rode up. She got one of Callum's slugs in the shoulder. I loaned him my horse to take her to town. Mine would carry double weight easier and town was nearer than coming here.'

A trickle of sweat ran down Donovan's cheek as he watched the doubts expressed on Sam's face. Then Stevens snapped the question.

'If all that is true, why all the lies in the first place?'

'You had a gun pointed at me and you mightn't have believed that I'd bring you the news. Things being the way they are between us.'

'You're damned right I wouldn't have believed you and I don't know that I do now.'

Stevens moved his horse closer to Donovan and his left hand unhooked the lariat from his saddle. With a deft move he slipped the noose over the rancher's head and settled it round his neck.

'Now ride to town and make it fast. If you've any notions

of breaking loose, forget 'em unless you want to be dragged by the neck.'

Donovan turned and settled the reins in his grip. Sweat ran freely down his face now and the loosely fitted rope about his great bull neck seemed to be already constricting his breathing. He felt, as he urged the mare to a fast trot, that unless some miracle happened, the rope about his neck would be a hangman's noose. Then he thought of Hennesey and his spirits lifted a little. Hennesey would not stand for lynch-law, even if Lucy had died as a result of the shot. The rancher pushed the mare to a faster pace. The sooner he got to town the better the chance that the girl still lived.

The arrival in the town of the pair on horses that were blowing heavily brought men running after them and quite a few yelled out instructions for Stevens to get his end of the lariat over the branch of a tree. The stir made Judge Bohun heave himself from his chair on the porch of his house. He stared for a moment then hurried towards the Silver Dollar where Donovan and Stevens were climbing from their saddles. Bohun had not been inside the saloon since the abortive election for a marshal, both Belle and Luke Carter having told him plainly that his presence would not be tolerated. Now, however, he hurried up the steps of the veranda, as did a dozen other men, curious to learn how Donovan came to have a rope round his neck. Bohun's hurry to get inside the saloon was not entirely prompted by curiosity. There was in his mind some glimmering of an idea of making profit for himself out of Donovan's situation. Bohun had heard a garbled account of Lucy being carried into the saloon, had seen Johnnie Callum ride Donovan's horse out of town and the quick following up of Hennesey and Carter, and already the sequence of events were adding up to something near the truth in Bohun's mind. The main thing was, Donovan was in serious trouble and Donovan was a man well able to pay those who helped him.

Belle was saying to Stevens when Bohun made his way towards them: 'I think she's going to be all right, Sam. There's some fever but it's not getting any worse.'

Men crowded forward to hear her words, Bohun among them. She gave them a brief glance then went on. 'Johnnie's gone gunning for this skunk although it seems from what Johnnie said that Lucy getting the slug was an accident.'

Stevens viewed Donovan sourly. 'You can get that rope off your neck though I reckon I'll be hunting you if my sister dies.'

Sam allowed the end of the lariat to drop and was sliding his gun back in its holster when a man pushed forward and gave a savage snatch to the end of the rope.

'Friends of mine were shot down in the street on account of this guy. I say we ought to hang him while we got the chance.'

Donovan grabbed at the tightening noose about his neck and using all his great strength hauled backwards until the other man was nearly off his feet. The rancher bellowed a curse and somehow that, more than the action of the man at the other end of the rope, brought anger to the rest of the men. A dozen hands gripped on the rope and jerked Donovan off his feet. Sam's hand went towards his gun as the rancher was dragged across the sawdust covered floor to the batwings. More men were pushing into the place and cries of, 'String the murdering skunk up,' came from all sides. Sam was still hesitating to draw his gun, divided between a love of justice and a hatred for the man who had been the cause of so much trouble and bloodshed. Bohun was finding himself shouldered to one side, but his eyes were still on the struggling, mountain of a man on the floor, and his mind on the fact that Donovan alive might mean profit for himself.

Bohun moved quickly, heaving his bulk of fat along at

speed he had not known in years. He pushed behind the bar, passed the pop-eyed bartender and grabbed the shot-gun that hung beneath the mirror. With the double-barrelled weapon levelled at the shouting men he yelled out:

'Hold it, all of you, or I'll fill you full of shot.'

'You damned, interfering old fool,' Belle shouted as the crowd of men dropped the rope and backed away from the wide muzzles of the gun, 'can't you see he'll ride you into the dust when it suits him?'

Sam gripped her arm. 'You wouldn't want to see a man lynched, Belle.'

She turned on him furiously. 'The hell I wouldn't! I'd like to see the louse swing higher than a kite.'

She stamped away and climbed the stairs, her full skirts swirling angrily.

Donovan had got to his feet and taken the rope from his neck. His limbs were trembling slightly and sweat poured down his near purple face. Bohun still held the shot-gun directed at the men, but now he had allowed the weight of the barrels to rest on the bar. He, too, was trembling, shocked by his own efforts. Stevens eyed the men grouped about the batwings. A few looked sheepish but rage burned in the eyes of at least half-a-dozen and it seemed to him that only a little spark was wanted to inflame them further. Donovan moved towards the bar, brushing sawdust from his clothes as he walked.

'I'll take that shot-gun, Bohun,' he said thickly, 'and thanks for the help.'

Sam whipped out his Colt. 'Keep your hands off that gun, Donovan.'

Donovan turned and glared at him, then there was a shuffling movement as a few men slid out through the batwings.

'I need a gun to get out of here alive,' Donovan snarled.

'You're darned right you do,' came from a straggly moustached man at the batwings. 'You'll need a gun and a hoss and we'll see that there ain't any hoss. Come on, fellers, we can wait outside for this guy. We've got plenty of time.'

Sam turned the gun on the speaker. 'That's wild talk, Jeff Richards, and you know it. I've suffered as much as anyone from Donovan's rough riding but I don't want to see lynch-law in the town. Donovan will leave here on my horse and there'll be no shooting in the back as he goes. We still have Hennesey as marshal. Remember that. Bohun, put that shot-gun back where it belongs. Donovan, make for the batwings and get on your way.'

The men crowding the front of the batwings looked at one another uncertainly then drifted out of the place. Stevens followed closely and Donovan, with an effort at recovering his shattered dignity was close behind him. Bohun remained behind the bar and with hands that shook poured himself a large sized whiskey. Outside, Donovan mounted in silence, feeling the glare of angry eyes upon him. He had no sense of gratitude towards Stevens for making his escape possible and felt only a little for Bohun's saving of his life. As he swung away from the place, his thought centred mainly on the run of ill luck he had had. He should, by now, have run Hennesey out of town, wiped out that young upstart, Callum, and have cleaned the Stevens' place out. Yet here he was on a horse loaned to him by a man who had good cause to hate him thoroughly, his holster empty and at his back, in his own town, a gang of yapping men who had wanted to string him up. String him up! By God, he'd show them who was the big boss in these parts. And before another day was over too. A big raid on the town was what was needed. A real shooting up then a follow-on to the Stevens' place. That would settle things. To hell with this notion of proving to himself that he was as good single handed as he had ever been. The years

132

were piling on him and there was no sense in denying the fact. He bent over the horse's neck and urged and spurred it to a punishing pace, took a bend in the trail at such a pace that he narrowly missed colliding with an aged wagon that creaked slowly along under the efforts of a pair of weary looking horses and passed on without giving heed to the curses hurled at him by the driver of the wagon. He had reached his house and was climbing from the saddle when it occurred to him that there had been something vaguely familiar about the face of the middle-aged man who had been driving the wagon. Still, he had only caught a blurred glimpse of the face, so it could have been that of one of the hundreds he had seen about the town. Nevertheless, as he went indoors and bawled for the cook boy to go and fetch Stone, he had some difficulty in dismissing the matter from his mind. He had lighted and a quarter smoked a cigar before it occurred to him that the boy had been gone a long time and again a sense of unease gripped him. He strode into the hall with the intention of seeing for himself what was keeping the boy, then he remembered his empty holster and returned to the living-room. He was in the act of loading a weapon for himself when he heard the boy in the hall. He holstered the gun and stepped into the hall. The cook's face was covered in blood and it took Donovan a full minute to understand from the boy's pidgin English that the bunkhouse was full of fighting men.

The fighting had spread to the outside of the bunkhouse when he reached it, with eight men punching away at each other indiscriminately.

'Let up, you scum,' Donovan shouted, then had to jump to one side as a ninth man came spinning through the doorway and sprawled to the ground. He seized the man by the shoulder as he was getting up.

'What's it all about?'

The puncher shook free from his grasp. 'Darned if I know,' and then plunged into the bunkhouse again.

Donovan punched and shoved those still outside into something like order, then stepped into the bunkhouse. He guessed, as he entered the sweat stinking atmosphere of the place, that he had an ordinary bunkhouse row on his hands. Some quarrel over a poker game, most likely, and one that Stone should have quelled immediately. The long, narrow building seemed packed with struggling men and the gloom of the place resounded to grunts and curses as bodies thumped against the double tier of bunks.

The rancher bawled orders to break up the riot, but his words went unheeded and it was doubtful if his presence was noticed until, with a bellow of rage, he seized on the man nearest the door and threw him bodily through the opening. After that, he picked on men with deliberation, flinging some out of doors and clubbing others with the barrel of his gun. He made out Stone, at the further end of the cabin, backed against the cook-stove and swinging an iron skillet with his left hand. He began to fight towards the foreman, then a gun exploded, its thunder roaring above the rest of the din and Stone's head and shoulders were no longer visible to Donovan. The racket of sound died down as if a lid had been clamped on it and a lane between men suddenly stretched in front of Donovan. A narrow lane at the end of which a puncher named Rourke stood with a smoking gun in his hand and Stone's body at his feet. In the brooding silence that was now heavy on the place, Donovan and Rourke stared at one another. Both men had guns in their hands and each had defined the other's intention. Rourke stood stiffly watchful, the gun hanging down by his side but his grip on the butt hard and tense. Donovan's stance was easier, his feet a little apart, the hand that held the Colt was a little to the back of his massive thigh and his big thumb was working slowly to raise the hammer of the weapon without the loud click that would come from a rapid movement. The next few seconds, he know, would bring death to one of them and he intended that if possible his own gun would be just the fraction of a second in front of Rourke's that would give him the advantage. The difference in time between a gun already cocked and that of a weapon whose hammer had to lift before it could fall.

Rourke's hand made the smallest of preliminary moves and in that moment, Donovan gave a sideways twist to his body, his gun arm came up and the thumbed back hammer dropped on the shell. Rourke lifted on his feet, his gun came up, exploded uselessly, then dropped from his hand. For the briefest space of time he maintained an impossible looking forward droop of his body, then his knees folded and he rolled half on top of Stone.

Donovan gave a swift intaking of breath as if air had been long cut off from him. So he could still shoot straight and the business with Lucy Stevens and young Callum had been just bad luck. In full command of himself again he barked a question.

'What the hell's it all about? You, Red Hanlon, answer up for the rest.'

Hanlon looked at him woodenly. 'I don't have to, mister, I ain't workin' for you now. I've just quit.'

He turned around and began to gather gear together from his bunk. Other men followed his example. Donovan viewed the scene with growing irritation.

'Well, one of you speak up. Don't act like a lot of dummies.'

Hanlon turned on him savagely. 'Dummies is what we've been. Here, look at this.'

Donovan came forward as Hanlon whipped a blanket from a bunk and disclosed a dead man.

'That's Rube Edgars,' Hanlon went on angrily. 'Got a slug in him at that blasted affair in the town. Lain here for days without any attention 'cept what us fellers gave him when we'd done workin'. Rube died in the middle of the night an' some of us were fixin' to take time this mornin' to bury him decent. But Stone, darn his hide, says no. There's no time to waste, so we've just got to dig a bit of a hole an' toss Rube in it then scrape the ground flat again. That's what started the ruckus, so now you can do what the hell you like with Stone, we're taking Edgars an' Rourke to town with us an' havin' them buried decent.'

'I suppose you have your own wagon ?' Donovan said ominously.

'We haven't. We're going to borrow one of yours. Your gun is still in your hand if you want to argue matters.'

Donovan gave a slight start. He had forgotten the Colt was still in his grip. He glanced about and saw at least twenty pairs of eyes staring hard at him, and suddenly he was aware that the empire he had built on gunplay was crumbling before his eyes all because gunthrowing, fast riding, range hands held to some mawkish sentiment when it came to the burying of one of their number. He said with a growl:

'Borrow a wagon if you want to and get to hell out of here.'

'We were going to,' Hanlon growled back.

Somehow, Donovan managed to retain what little of his temper was left and he swung about and walked out of the bunkhouse. He planted himself on a chair on the veranda of the house and chewed at an unlit cigar. In the red glow of the setting sun he saw the wagon roll away from the bunkhouse with a long string of riders behind it. He counted thirty-two figures silhouetted against the sky-line and began to wonder uneasily how many men were left to him and of those that were left, what proportion were fighters. The sun dipped and he threw away the pulped cigar, took another from his pocket and lighted it, then sat brooding on. The sudden quitting of the men was a blow, and not only to his aggressive plans. He was now desperately short of men to work his vast herds. How long before he could recruit more? Weeks, more likely months. There was little he could do in the matter beyond telling stage and freight drivers that he needed riders and letting them spread the news in their normal exchanges. They would make other talk too, and not the kind that was likely to attract ordinary range hands to the MD spread.

Donovan tossed away the cigar and went indoors. Men he must have and as quickly as possible. Fall round-up time was less than a month away and if he had not men to handle the round-up and the subsequent drive to the railhead, even his finances would be strained to the limit. Indoors, the problem of men magnified itself to even greater proportions. He saw his mighty herds untended and wandering freely after a miserably diminished round-up and drive. Then would come the Spring with calves crowding the already packed ranges, producing enough mavericks to make wholesale rustling profitable and legal for every range tramp that cared to take a hand in the business.

CHAPTER TWELVE

In the last of the daylight Johnnie, Hennesey and Carter looped the reins of their weary mounts over the hitchrail of the Silver Dollar and, beating the dust from their clothes, entered the place. Johnnie's face was dark with anger at his failure to locate Donovan, first at, or on the way to, Chimney Rock and later at the Stevens' place. Hennesey's face showed relief at not having been present at yet another killing, and Carter felt the same at not having to display his lack of skill with a gun. Johnnie had a fixed idea in his head. One that neither of the other two could shake. He would get a fresh horse and ride out to Donovan's place. However, he wanted news of Lucy first, and for that reason only had he entered the place.

Seeing Sam in the bar was no surprise to any one of the three, but Sam's rapidly told story of Donovan's latest moves brought sharp comment. Hennesey expressed relief that a lynching had been avoided. Carter seemed uncertain whether to be glad or sorry, but Johnnie's opinion was undivided and emphatic.

'You should have let the murdering bastard hang.'

The words shaped oddly on Johnnie's lips, and after an interval he said: 'I'm goin' to the livery for a boss. Jus' wanted to know how Lucy was before I went.'

The last sentence came in a voice so harsh and cracked that Stevens guessed at something more than ordinary, sympathetic enquiry. He said softly:

'I was about to go upstairs and ask myself. Belle's been with her this last hour. Why don't you go up and find out? The second door on the left.'

'Me – go upstairs and ask?'

'Sure, why not? Lucy'll be glad to know you enquired when she wakes up.'

Johnnie eyed the carpet-covered stairs and cream painted banister, then glanced down at his dust-caked clothing.

'I'm not sorta dressed for goin' up a place like that.'

Carter smiled. 'There's nothing you can hurt there, Johnnie. The carpet will brush easily enough.'

Johnnie nodded and climbed the stairs. He found himself on a cream painted landing and stood hesitant before the door Sam had indicated. With its smooth finish the door seemed, to him, the very last word in tasteful luxury. Its colour was cool and restful, not exciting like the garish colours in the saloon. He found himself wanting to own such a door. To be able to turn the knob of it and open it whenever he wished. To pass through and find, on the other side – Johnnie wrenched himself from the dream that was forming in his mind, and knocked gently.

The door opened a little and showed a rectangle of wall-paper above Belle's head. She gave him a fleeting smile.

'She's about the same, Johnnie, though the fever might be a bit less.'

Johnnie's rage against Donovan came back in full force. 'I'll be on my way then, Belle. Just came into town for a fresh horse. I guess the feller in the livery will let me have one.'

'Charge it to me, Johnnie, though I'm not saying you're doing the best thing in going to Donovan's place. That's where you're going, isn't it?'

'That's right. I thought you wanted him dead as much as I do.'

Belle nodded. 'I do, Johnnie, and I feel no shame for thinking that way, but Donovan on his own ground is a mighty big chore. I wouldn't want you to be the one to get killed.' Her green eyes regarded him for a moment, then she went on: 'Johnnie, I've not known you for long but I've gotten to like you. Don't go getting yourself killed.'

He looked at her woodenly. 'So long as I get that big skunk I don't care what happens to me. He shot Lucy and—'

'You think a whole lot of Lucy, don't you?' Belle cut in.

'Sure, she's been nice to me. Sam has as well. I like Sam a whole lot.'

'You like me, too, and Ed, and Luke, but not in the way you like Lucy.'

Johnnie reddened. 'There isn't more than one way to like anyone, is there?'

'I think you're beginning to know differently. In fact, I'm not sure if you aren't trying to lie to me—' She broke off as the beat of a number of hoofs reached their ears. 'Lord! not Donovan's crowd again. Wait, I can see from this window.'

She whisked away from the door and was back in a few seconds. 'It's them all right. Twenty at the least and with a wagon. Hell, I might have known it'd be something like this.'

Johnnie was already moving towards the stairs. 'We'll hold them down some way or other, Belle.'

'You're damned right we will. I'm coming with you.'

Johnnie raised a hand as if to push her back into the room. 'Look after Lucy. I'm getting pretty handy with this Colt. I reckon if I stay at the head of the stairs, I'll have the jump on anyone below.'

He reached the head of the stairs and looked down. A bunch of men, some of whom he recognised as Donovan's, were grouped about Carter, Stevens and Hennesey. He could hear the hum of their conversation but as yet there seemed no sign of trouble. He went cautiously down three of the steps and stood with the Colt in his hand, then to his surprise the Donovan men turned away and walked out of the saloon.

Johnnie came down the stairs. 'I thought we were all set for another fight.'

Hennesey noted the gun in his hand. 'There might be one yet. There's been one on Donovan's place. Donovan's shot and killed one of his own men. They've brought the feller to town to have him buried decently. Seems the trouble blew up over fixing a funeral for another feller.'

Johnnie listened to the remainder of the tale then in a puzzled tone, said:

'Why should that make for more trouble here? A split among Donovan's men is just about what is wanted.' He slid the Colt into its holster. 'I ought to have a better chance of getting at that guy now. It'll be plenty dark when I get there. Most likely, what men are left on the place will be in the bunkhouse and—'

Hennesey gripped his arm. 'Johnnie, don't do it. Calling a man out to fight is just another kind of murder. That is, if you win out. In any case I was counting on your help in here.'

'Don't see that you need any,' Johnnie said roughly, 'and there's one thing certain. There'll be no end to shooting and killing as long as Donovan is alive.'

'We figure that those men of Donovan's will be back here as soon as they get the funeral business over,' Stevens said. 'They'll get to hard drinking and when that happens its difficult to say which way their tempers will go. It's possible that some of them will get to thinking that they're without jobs and—'

Johnnie cut him short. 'I've got it figured, Sam. You and Ed want to stop me from going after Donovan. You reckon

I'll get myself killed. Well, that isn't so important so long as I get Donovan and, raw or not at this gunfighting business, I'll do just that.'

Carter nodded. 'Somehow, I think you will, Johnnie. It's true that we weren't really expecting Donovan's crowd to cut loose—'

'I'm goin' to the livery to get a horse,' Johnnie broke in. He swung towards the batwings, saw that a middle-aged man was pushing through them and paused to give him a clear way. The man came straight towards him, stared at him for a moment then said hesitantly:

'You Johnnie Callum?'

Johnnie's eyes travelled quickly from the greying hair that showed under the battered Stetson, down the length of the stringy, work-worn figure and came back to look straight into the slightly faded blue eyes.

'Yes, I'm Johnnie Callum.'

'My name's Seth Callum.'

'Seth Callum?' Johnnie said without expression.

'Your Paw, son.'

'Paw!' Johnnie stared at the man, saw an underlying sadness in the blue eyes and was at the same time aware of the drawing near of the three men he had just been talking to. He could sense their surprise, even feel that there was some kind of emotion in Sam Stevens and knew that he ought to feel some himself. But there was none in him, surprise, yes, but of other feeling there was simply nothing. He knew that he ought to say something to this man who claimed to be his father. Express doubt, or if he believed the man, show pleasure. No, more than pleasure, something much, much stronger. He ought to feel towards this stranger the way he felt to – to Lucy.

'Hello, Paw, glad to see you.' It was all Johnnie could offer. That and a handshake. Then, after an awkward interval:

'Maw, is she around here, some place?'

Again he struggled against the sense that there ought to have been feeling in the question, but it had been like asking a man what shape his herd was in. A polite enquiry without any real interest in the answer. Then came the reply and he had feeling in plenty.

'You Maw's dead, Johnnie. Someone's slug got her the night Donovan cleared us off our place. We were shoved in our old wagon an' she started to run screaming to find you. I don't say the shot was aimed at her but it got her just the same. She died about sunup an' I went near crazy, thought you'd gone down the same way. I roamed the hills about our place for days, lookin' for your body an' finally when I gave up I went the other side of Leastown. I never heard a word about you until a week ago when I was told about some kind of a fight between this town an' Donovan an' your name was mentioned. I came to see for myself. I left the trail an' went to the old place by the rock an' I saw the stakes you'd driven in an' the notices pinned on them. Johnnie, you can't stop Donovan with notices.'

'Paw.' Johnnie gripped the elder Callum's arm forcibly. 'I don't aim to stop Donovan with notices. I'm fixin' to do it with bullets. Was on my way to his place when you walked in. Now I've got to be honest with you. I can't remember either you or Maw. I can remember the night Donovan came all right and the things that happened to me after, but nothin' about you or Maw, but I've seen him gun a woman down with a slug that was aimed at me an' when I give him his I'll try an' think I'm doin' it for Maw.'

'Lord, son. Your Maw wouldn't have wanted you to go gunnin' on her account. She hated guns.' Seth Callum turned to Hennesey. 'Mister, you're the marshal. Tell him that this shooting men down is no good.'

Hennesey shook his head. 'It won't work, Mr Callum.

143

We've tried to put Johnnie off the idea but he's his own man now, and set with the idea that the only way of dealing with Donovan is to kill him.'

'It is the only way,' Belle's voice came from the foot of the stairs, 'Mr Callum, I'm glad to know you. I've been standing here listening to your story. You stay right here with us and let Johnnie go and do what he must.'

As she came towards them agitation showed on Seth Callum's face. He met Belle's green eyes with a pleading look and from them seemed to draw resolution. He turned his gaze on Johnnie.

'Son, I'll wait here for you. Maybe you have got the right idea. Others have tried law on Donovan and got no satisfaction from it.'

Johnnie nodded and went towards the batwings. The arrival of his father had shaken him more than he realized and the fact that up to now he could feel no affection worried him. He even had a sense of guilt over the way he felt about his mother's death. He was angry about it but he did not feel the same burning rage that he had over the shooting of Lucy. That was the thing that was driving him to go after Donovan. In fact, and he might just as well admit it to himself, he wanted to murder Donovan and did not care whether the rancher had a chance to defend himself or not. Once he got that far with his thinking the other things cluttering his mind seemed to become insignificant. The coming of his father, the news of his mother's death, the growing idea that both Hennesey and Sam Stevens might be cowards where Donovan was concerned, all faded in the light of this new conception. He was going to kill Donovan because the man had put Lucy's life in danger.

It was practically dark when he came out of the livery astride a powerfully built black, and a quarter moon hung low in the sky. For finding his way to Donovan's ranch he would have to trust partly to luck and partly to information he had picked up. He followed the main trail for the best part of half an hour and all the time his rage against Donovan burned furiously so that his temples began to pound and a red mist form before his eyes. His mind floated hazily. Josh Manders came into his thoughts and he lived again the moments when his fingers were clawed in the man's hair and he was pounding the sheepherder's head against the ground. Then it was Stone, until Lucy had stopped him. Her name, muttered to himself, brought remembrance of her thrusting the rifle into his hands and the calmly given advice on how to use it. She was always like that, calm and cool, cool as shaded river water. He had to be that way himself if he was going to kill Donovan.

Suddenly, he was aware of rain. Big, isolated spots that plopped on the brim of his hat or splashed widely on his hands holding the reins. Next, he heard the rumble of thunder and an upwards glance showed moon and stars effaced. Clear thinking came to him again and as his eyes searched for the side trail that led to the MD spread, the magnitude of the job he had undertaken appalled him. Fear grew as he contemplated what was before him. Not fear for himself but fear that he might fail and so leave Lucy in further peril from Donovan. His thoughts included others in that peril. Sam Stevens, Luke Carter, Hennesey, perhaps, and of course his own father, but they were vague figures compared to Lucy.

In drenching rain and to the increasing sound of thunder, he came to a side trail. It was stamped out nearly as widely as the main trail and a large notice-board gave the information that it led to the MD house. Three miles down the side trail a swing gate barred his way and he got from a sodden saddle into squelching mud to open it. Mounted again and dripping water, he came at last to the house. A shadowy, sprawling structure, seen vaguely through the lancing rain. He left the saddle again and was moving forward on foot when deafening thunder accompanied by blinding forks of lightning shocked him to a standstill. For seconds, the house stood illuminated in its ugliness of red stone and yellow clay pointing, apparently on fire with vivid blue light. He had time enough to note the house's main details – before the darkness shut down again and the rain sheeting in front of him cut off even the outline of the building. In another few minutes he reached the shelter of the veranda and stood there wringing the weight of water from his hat. He felt cold in his drenched clothes and water pulped boots, but the desire to come to grips with Donovan was as strong as ever and it seemed to him that the storm was in his favour. There had been no more lightning since that one blinding flare and the roll of the thunder was now distant again, but the rain sheeted down even more heavily; an effective cut off from whatever men were in the bunkhouse. He felt around for, and found, the catch of the screen door and stepped inside the hall. There he paused and drew the Colt from a holster that felt like wet rag. He felt the weight of the weapon in his hand, then a clammy sweat broke out on his forehead. He knew very little about guns. Had the torrents of water had any effect upon the Colt? Before he had time to decide he heard footsteps overhead. Heavy footsteps, like he would expect to hear from Donovan. The steps seemed to be coming downstairs, though in the blackness of the hall he could not see. The movement ceased and to his strained hearing came the small sounds of a man breathing. He remembered his own breathing and it sounded noisy. He tried to still it, then Donovan's voice boomed.

'Whoever you are, skulking there, you'd better shout out before I fill this place with lead.'

Johnnie steadied the Colt in the direction of Donovan's

voice. 'Johnnie Callum, I've come for you, Donovan.'

Donovan's gun flashed red flame and Johnnie dropped to the floor, pulling the trigger as he went down. There was a click from the hammer but no explosion, then Donovan's gun spattered lead all around him. He counted the shots mentally and after the sixth came up from the floor and charged in the direction he had seen the gun flashes come from. He had a blurred impression of Donovan moving quickly towards an oblong of lesser darkness that he knew must be the door, and a moment later they were both outside and moving blindly through the sheeting rain.

Donovan's movements were in the vague direction of the bunkhouse and help. He was sloshing through ankle-deep mud and cursing his luck at not being able to hit Callum with one of the six shots fired in the comparatively small space of the hall, cursing also what he believed to be a fact. Callum, for all his inexperience as a gun fighter, had held his fire until he was certain of a killing shot.

Johnnie floundered through the mud without a plan in his head. He guessed that Donovan would make for the bunkhouse but had no idea of its direction. The thunder began to roll again, blanketing the small sounds made by both men. Then a flicker of lightning gave momentary illumination. It was gone before Johnnie could get any advantage from it, but it showed Donovan that he himself was progressing towards one side of the bunkhouse rather than to it. He moved in the new direction and, as he did so, thunder crashed and reverberated directly overhead. With it came both sheet and fork lightning showing everything in sharp brilliance. It showed Donovan that Johnnie, gun in hand, was nearer to the bunkhouse than he was himself. It also gave him a sharpened view of a black horse, already saddled and trembling with fear of the storm. Donovan ran with mud-laden feet for the horse, expecting that the gun in

Callum's hand would blast at any moment. Darkness and silence, except for the lashing of the rain, came again. Johnnie had seen all of the big ranger's movements, he had also seen a corral with thirty or forty horses milling about in an effort to find shelter. He found the sliprail by some stroke of luck and throwing it to one side grabbed at one of the darkly moving forms in the corral. The horse, half mad with fear, streaked out of the place with Johnnie hanging to its mane and neck. He gave several swings before he reached its back then could do nothing but cling like a burr until the animal ran off its terror. For minutes the horse kept up a maddened pace, with Johnnie having no sense of the direction it was taking. He was on the point of throwing himself from its back as being useless to continue when the sheeting rain ceased as suddenly as if it had been turned off at a tap. Seeing became possible and less than ten yards in front of him was the big gate, flung wide open. It had to be Donovan who had left it like that, yet he wondered why when he and the horse hurtled through it. A man of Donovan's sense would surely have stopped his mount the moment he was covered by the darkness, reloaded his gun and stayed nearer home where there was a possibility of help coming to him. Then Johnnie remembered something that had happened in the hall. As he had come up from the floor after Donovan's last shot something had whirled past him and thudded against a wall. That could have been Donovan's gun, thrown in a last attempt to stop Johnnie himself. The idea brought a warming glow to his shivering body. When he came up with Donovan it would be hand to hand for he had no idea of how to make his own Colt useful again quickly.

With the cessation of the rain, Donovan pulled up. Hatless and coatless and with the rest of his water soaked clothing sticking to his body, he cursed himself for having run so far. Although he had been fool enough to leave himself without a gun, at least he had what must be Callum's horse. Now that the sky was clearing a little he could swing away from the trail and come back to his own fence somewhere near the bunkhouse, leave his mount and climb through the fence and rouse the sleeping men. Even if Callum did sight him it would be easy to keep out of gun range seeing that Callum was on foot. Donovan swung his mount to leave the trail then quickly turned it again at the sound of horse's hoofs. He got one glimpse of Johnnie, head down over his mount's neck, then rammed spurs at an already blowing horse and sent it streaking towards the main trail and the town.

He needed a gun, needed it desperately, and the only place he could think of was Judge Bohun's house.

CHAPTER THIRTEEN

With the last of the rainstorm a sheepherder crawled from underneath the rag of canvas that served as a tent. It was Josh Manders, the man whom Johnnie believed he had killed. Manders stared about, bleary eyed from last night's whiskey, and in the light of pre-dawn saw little but water. It was everywhere. Running in new river courses between the rocks, making depressions into small lakes and turning any soft ground into oozing mud. All would be clear in a few hours, but in the meantime, sheep that had not already drowned were crowding each other for what little dry land remained. Manders knew that if he were to save the rest of his flock he must drive them uphill towards the main trail some three miles distant, then through the town and out on the other side. He disliked the prospect. Gathering and driving sheep in the half light would be bad enough, but moving them along the trail would be dangerous. There were Donovan's men, for one thing. He knew he could expect no mercy from them. Then there was this kid, Callum. Suppose he should meet with him in the town? Unlikely, because it would barely be dawn when he reached the place, but he had heard that the youngster had become tough and something of a fighter. Manders scowled. There was only one way of dealing with tough youngsters. He rolled up his piece of canvas, stowing

150

the dirt-grimed blankets and cooking gear in the roll, drained the whiskey bottle, then saddled the sway-backed horse he owned. Before mounting he spent some time in cleaning and loading his shot-gun.

Working the sheep was even worse than he had expected. The main trail had become a quagmire with the wheel ruts a foot deep and yard-wide rivers. Sheep bogged down frequently and his horse did little better, so that the town was fully astir when he reached it. There, on the better drained ground, the flock broke and scattered, running between shacks and trampling down vegetable patches and bringing their owners cursing and shouting to the scene. Somehow, the flock was reformed in front of the Silver Dollar and Manders started to harry them forward again to the accompaniment of curses from half the population. He turned in his saddle to give answer to one more than ordinary lurid oath and as he did so his spine went rigid with fear. Donovan, pushing a mud-spattered black horse to its uttermost was not more than thirty yards behind him and distant by another twenty yards was young Callum. Manders put the only construction his half frozen mind would fit to the scene. The pair had ganged together and were coming for him.

Donovan had halved the distance to Manders and was cursing at the flock of sheep between himself and safety when he saw the shotgun go up to the sheepherder's shoulder. He made a desperate effort to send the horse into a swerve and the moment before the gun roared, glimpsed Hennesey, among others, on the saloon veranda and Bohun on his own porch, then his horse floundered and rolled sideways. Donovan hit the ground with a bone-jarring crash but, conscious of the peril behind him, was up instantly and running towards the saloon. He saw Manders fire again, then Hennesey rush at the man and wrest the gun from his hands. In the next second sheep seemed to be all about him, their

151

smelly bodies pressing against his legs and hampering his movement. He gave a glance over his shoulder and saw Callum, sliding from his horse's back, his passage blocked solidly with the sheep. Callum was a bare twenty yards away but his gun was still in its holster. The fact spurred Donovan to greater effort. Evidently the youngster could not trust his marksmanship at even this range. The way to Bohun's house suddenly cleared and he took it at a panting run. He grabbed the astonished judge by the shoulder.

'Your gun, man. Quick!'

Donovan's hand darted beneath the long skirts of Bohun's coat and wrenched the .45 from its holster. He made a quick check on the loading and stepped to the middle of the street.

Johnnie saw the whole of the business and ceased his struggling to get forward. He stood, hemmed in by hundreds of bleating, struggling sheep, and suddenly he felt very tired. Hennesey, who was still holding Manders and had dragged him to the side of the street, looked very small and distant. Belle, his father and Carter, on the veranda of the Silver Dollar were puppets, still and lifeless. Only Donovan was real as the sixgun in his hamlike fist.

Donovan's voice came booming. 'Callum, pull that gun, damn you. I'm not going to have it said that I shot you down without giving you a chance.'

Johnnie hesitated momentarily then slowly drew the Colt. He stood for a fraction of a second with the useless weapon pointed at the ground. In the moment of time he imagined was left to him he still thought of somehow getting Donovan and making the world safe for Lucy. He raised the muzzle of the gun and in that instant, Donovan fired. The slug slammed into Johnnie's left shoulder and spun him half round, the movement of the sheep about his legs dropping him floundering amongst them. He was aware of a burning pain and of the close contact of warm, wool covered bodies. He got half to his feet and Donovan's gun roared again, three times. Hot blood spurted over him but somehow he got to his feet. Donovan, he thought, had not yet succeeded in killing him. If only he could stay alive until he got his hands on the man. Like he had got them on Manders. But Manders wasn't dead. Queer about that, he'd been scared about what he had done to the sheepherder and there wasn't any reason for the scare. No reason either why Donovan shouldn't kill him with one of the two remaining shells that were in his gun. A woman screamed loudly as he pushed slowly through the sheep, and Johnnie grinned to himself. He must look one hell of a sight with all this smother of blood on him. But now he knew that most of it was sheep's blood. All of it in fact except that coming from the hole in his left shoulder. Only a small hole, and it didn't burn very much now. Sheep! Hell take the stinking things. They seemed all over and Donovan's gun was levelled at him again. Fifteen paces. There could be no miss at that distance. The bang and the spurt of flame came but no shock of the slug smashing into bone and flesh. Donovan had missed and he might do so again with those woollies bumping against his legs. Now he was backing up, trying to get clear of the sheep for a steady shot. The last one in the gun. It was enough to make anyone laugh. This great giant of a man, gun in hand, backing away from an unarmed man. But no one was laughing. From the corner of his eye he could see those on the saloon veranda, all frozen faced except Belle, and hers was working spasmodically, as if she were trying to shout something. Donovan had stopped backing up, was glancing about to see that he was clear of sheep. Belle's voice screamed.

'Johnnie! For Chris'sake. The gun! Shoot, blast you.'

Johnnie's memory jerked to the fact that the Colt was still in his hand. No wonder Donovan was backing from him. He raised the gun with a sudden swing and sent it hurtling. It smashed straight into Donovan's face, who at the very moment, triggered off his last shot. Half stunned and almost blinded by a flow of blood from his forehead he staggered about, tripped and went down. As he got to his feet, Johnnie was upon him, hands clawing for, and finding, a hold on the rancher's massive neck. Donovan's big hands grabbed at Johnnie's wrists in an effort to break the hold and for seconds the pair rocked on their feet in the fierceness of their combat. The silence that had held the watchers broke and men and women surged forward from every angle. Sheep scattered with frightened bleats, collected again in small bunches, then suddenly the whole flock broke in one direction and left a cleared space to the struggling men and the yelling, cheering onlookers.

Bohun found himself in the front line of the crowded circle and apprehension grew in his mind as he saw that Donovan, despite his giant stature, was unable to break the hold that Callum had on his neck. Suppose the fight ended in the death of the big man, how would things go for himself? Already, he was an outcast in the town. If Donovan should die he could see himself being hounded out of the town. There was a sudden surge forward of the crowd as Donovan, using all his strength and extra height, whirled Callum off his feet but, failing to break his hold, crashed with him to the ground. Bohun found himself isolated. He craned his neck to see who was uppermost of the pair and at that moment felt something hard in the mire at his feet. He knew instinctively that it was a gun and with a quick stoop for one of his bulk he snatched the weapon up. A hasty glance showed him that it was not the gun Donovan had wrenched from him, so it must be Callum's. The weight of it told him it was loaded, yet Callum had not tried to use it. His fingers clawed mud from around the action of the Colt, and as a roaring cheer went up from the crowd, he managed to make the chambers spin. He got a narrowed view of the struggling men. Callum was uppermost, his hands tightly on Donovan's throat. The big man's eyes were bulging, his tongue half out. Callum gave a mighty heave that jerked Donovan's shoulders from the ground and at that moment Bohun pulled the trigger then dropped the gun and rammed it into the mud with his foot.

It was a good enough shot from hip level but had not taken into account the movement of the two men. A movement that had suddenly ceased. Movement had ceased in the crowd too and silence had come.

Johnnie still had Donovan by the throat, but it was in a slackening hold now. He was staring at the big man's face and it was a moment before he realized that Donovan was dead. With the knowledge came revulsion and a feeling of great weakness. Slowly, he let the dead man's head drop to the ground, then got unsteadily to his feet. He had a feeling of being alone in spite of the crowd that surrounded him. Alone and unspeakably filthy with mud and blood, his own and Donovan's and that of the stinking sheep. He took a step away from the dead man and felt himself reeling. Then men were all around him, hands were supporting him, cheers sounded, but somehow they were very far off.

'Get this down you.' He recognised the voice as Belle's, the smell under his nose as whiskey, and drank from the glass that was pushed to his lips. He spluttered a little and gradually his eyes focused. He was at the top end of the saloon. The gaudy end, on one of the plush covered chairs, and Belle was grinning at him. A bowl of water was on the floor with a towel beside it. He felt clean again, strong too, except for the pain in his left shoulder. He made to stand up but a voice said:

'Not yet, son. You ain't fit to stand by a long way.' That was his Paw. The man he scarcely knew yet.

His eyes went from Belle's face to Carter's. Carter nodded and grinned. 'Belle's going to fix up the best room we've got so as you can rest up and get that shoulder wound of yours healed.'

Johnnie's mind went back to the fight. 'Who shot Donovan?'

'It's not been figured out yet. Hennesey's among the boys asking questions.' He gestured to where the marshal was talking to men at the bar. 'I guess most of us are hoping he won't get any answers.'

'Why so?'

'Well, I suppose it amounts to murder.'

'Would it have been murder if I'd killed Donovan myself? I was trying to hard enough.'

'You were fighting for your life, Johnnie. That's different.'

'Huh! I can't see any difference. Maybe the shot was intended for me. Maybe for Donovan. Whichever way it was, it saved one of our lives.'

Belle laughed. 'You should have been a lawyer, Johnnie. Now how about climbing into a bed?'

Johnnie shook his head. 'I want to talk to Hennesey. It ain't right for him to be huntin' the feller that saved my life.'

He got to his feet, brushing aside the hands outstretched to detain him. Hennesey swung round as he reached the bar.

'Johnnie, you oughtn't to be on your feet.'

'I'm OK. That looks like my Colt you've got in your hand.'

'It's yours, all right. Someone used it to fire the shot that killed Donovan.'

'Used that! It wouldn't shoot when I tried it. Anyway, I guess maybe I ought to be thankful to whoever fired it.'

'Feller deserves a medal,' a man observed.

'Or a rope around his neck,' Hennesey snapped. 'Anyone thought about who was doing best when the shot was fired? In any case it was plain murder.'

Sam Stevens pushed towards Hennesey. 'Ed, I wasn't going to say a word about what I saw, but you've got me thinking the shot wasn't intended for Donovan. I saw Bohun stoop and pick up a gun. It could have been that one. I don't know, I didn't see him use it.'

'We'll ask—' Hennesey began, but the rest of his words were drowned in an uproar of shouts to get Bohun and hang him.

In the concerted rush towards the batwings a voice yelled: 'Let's tar and feather him an' ride him on a rail. He's too darned heavy for a rope.'

Hennesey made a move to stop the ringleaders, but dozens of hands fended him roughly off and the yells to tar and feather Bohun outdid those in favour of hanging him.

Hennesey stood irresolute as the men poured into the street. He looked at Stevens as if for guidance or help, but Sam shook his head.

'You'll have to let them have their way, Ed. If you go out with a gun in your hand, you'll have to use it. Bohun isn't worth a lot of dead men. In any case, they aren't set on hanging him.'

'Ever seen a man tarred and feathered?' Hennesey asked grimly.

'No, I don't reckon I have.'

'It's worse than a hanging and usually the guy doesn't live to get over it.'

Johnnie's eyes went from one to the other. 'Then we've got to stop it.'

'How?' Hennesey snapped the word.

Johnnie grinned at him. 'I've been learnin' a feller can fight better without a gun than he can with one. Most guys won't draw on a feller who hasn't a gun. They won't lay hands on an injured man either.'

'They've got Bohun,' Sam cut in as a yell of triumph sounded from the street.

Johnnie moved towards the batwings. 'You fellers keep yourselves an' your guns out of sight,' he flung over his shoulder.

'I'm taking that order,' Hennesey growled to Stevens. 'The feller's a sight better man than I ever was, but just the same, a couple of rifles near the batwings might be handy.'

Belle, Carter and Seth Callum came hurrying forward.

'What's Johnnie up to now?' Belle demanded.

'Bring what rifles you have,' Hennesey snapped back, then to Seth Callum he said quietly: 'Seth, somehow you've raised a son who is a bigger man than any one of us in the town. Any two for that matter.'

In the street, Johnnie saw the mob collected outside the store. Bohun was head and shoulders above the crowd and even at this distance the abject fear on the man's face was distinguishable. Johnnie moved slowly up the street. He ached almost everywhere and the wound in his shoulder burned furiously. He reached the fringe of the crowd and a dozen voices shouted for a way to be cleared for him. He got to Bohun's side and saw the condition of the man. Already his clothing was torn to shreds and his face clawed and bleeding. He was astride and lashed to a fence rail held by half-a-dozen men. One of them grinned at him.

'Come to see the fun, Johnnie?'

'You could call it that, I guess.' Johnnie turned to a man who had been hammering in the top of a small barrel. 'What's in that?'

'Tar, Johnnie. Tar, to pour over the judge. Someone's gone to collect hen feathers. When they come we'll pour the lot over Bohun then ride him round the town on the rail before we throws him out. Everyone will be hurrahin' an' yellin' like mad. Be good fun for you to watch, Johnnie.'

'I'd as soon see him kickin' on the end of a rope an' I don't think that's fun either.'

The man got up from his crouch over the barrel. 'You mean to say you don't want nothin' done to this louse of a judge?'

'I mean I don't want anythin' like that done. In fact, if my shoulder weren't half busted, I'd lam into the feller who thought of the idea.'

'Well, I'll be doggone. Lookit here, Johnnie—'

'No. You listen to me.' Johnnie knew that in arguing with this one man he was arguing with the whole crowd of men. 'It seems to me that this town ain't got much gratitude. You was all wantin' Donovan put out of the way but none of you had the sand to go after him. One way or another, I fixed him an' I'd have killed him without Bohun hornin' in. I guess you know that.'

'Sure we do, but Bohun was trying to kill you.'

'Then I reckon I ought to have a say in what's to be done with him.'

'I reckon this town owes you that much, Johnnie,' a voice called out.

Johnnie's glance travelled over the whole of the crowd. He saw sheepishness, indifference, and on only a few faces, resentment.

'Lend me your knife, will you?' he said to the man beside the barrel.

The knife was handed over without a word. Johnnie made two quick slashes at the judge's bonds then said in a harsh voice:

'Get out of town and don't ever come back.'

'Some things from my house, Johnnie,' Bohun pleaded.

'You've got your life. That's more than you deserve. Be thankful.'

He watched a lane open in the crowd and the ragged, waddling figure of the judge pass down it, then he turned and on limbs that would scarcely support him, walked back to the Silver Dollar. Inside, he grinned faintly at his friends then looked directly at Belle.

'I ain't had time to ask until now, Belle. How's Lucy?'

'Doing grand, Johnnie. The fever's left her. You'd better

get into bed before it gets you.'

'Sure, I reckon I could sleep for a month.' He turned to his father. 'Paw, we'll get to know each other after I've had some sleep.'

'Sure, son. We've plenty of time, now.'

'The third room on the right, Johnnie,' Belle said crisply. 'Think you can make those stairs?'

'For a real bed I could make a hundred stairs.'

They watched him drag himself slowly up the stairs, then Carter said:

'So Donovan's empire is finally smashed. I wonder what will happen to his stuff?'

Hennesey shrugged. 'I'll have his house locked up in case there are any relatives, but the range beef will have to look after itself.'

'Hmm. That'll mean thousands of mavericks next spring. A darn good chance for anyone aimin' to start a herd,' said Stevens.

'That'd be a chance for Johnnie an' me,' Seth Callum put in eagerly.

Belle grinned. 'Don't you count on Johnnie being your second string, Paw Callum. I bet he'll start a herd all right, and I guess he'll let you work with him, but it'll be Mr and Mrs. Johnnie Callum's herd. You can bet on that.'

'Who is Johnnie figuring on marrying?' Hennesey asked in surprise.

'Johnnie isn't figuring it at all. I guess the notion hasn't entered his head. But it's in Lucy's all right, and that'll be good enough for both of them.'

Sam grinned at Seth. 'I guess you'd better come and fit in at my place. We wouldn't want to get in the way of Mr and Mrs Johnnie.'